The Lake
AT THE
End of the World

The Lake
AT THE
End of the World

Caroline Macdonald

DIAL BOOKS · New York

First published in the United States 1989 by Dial Books
A Division of Penguin Books USA Inc.
2 Park Avenue
New York, New York 10016

Published in Australia 1988
by Penguin Books Australia Ltd
Printed in the U. S. A.
First Edition
D
2 4 6 8 10 9 7 5 3 1

Library of Congress Cataloging in Publication Data
Macdonald, Caroline. The lake at the end of the world.
Summary: In 2025, in the wake of global environmental devastation,
the members of one surviving family encounter a teenaged boy
from a mysterious clandestine community.
[1. Science fiction.] I. Title.
PZ7.M14644Lak 1989 [Fic] 88-25678
ISBN 0-8037-0650-2

The Lake
AT THE
End of the World

PART
—1—

HECTOR STARTS THE STORY

They told me there was nothing left outside. They said the world was empty, finished.

The first time I go outside I believe them. I can see nothing. They forgot to tell me that the light outside is so brilliant, it is blinding.

I go outside again. For some reason, this time the light seems to be slowly disappearing. After a while my blindness lifts and I can see trees and other smaller plants of different kinds around a spread of flat ground. I don't leave the entrance to the caves. There are birds, I think. I can hear them singing, then gradually I can distinguish their movements against the colors of the trees.

The next time I take a few steps farther from the entrance. I watch the birds. Someone ages ago told me about the birds that live outside. Each time I go farther. Soon it is all I think about: the trip every day through the maze and out into the light.

I worry that someone will notice that I disappear regularly, perhaps follow me and stop me from coming here. They would never guess where I have gone.

It has always been unthinkable that anyone would try to leave the caves.

Sometimes I see another bird, larger and more brilliantly colored than the others. It hovers for a while, then curves slowly away and disappears into the distance. I cannot see this bird clearly because it remains in the sky. The light is too strong to look at the sky for more than a second. But I can tell that it is a very, very beautiful bird. It is the last thing I remember before I go to sleep at night. The brilliant blue wings drifting in the sky.

DIANA STARTS HER STORY

He was there again. He skulks in the shadows of the rocks and I suppose he thinks I can't see him. If the wind's right tomorrow I'll fly in closer. He can't be living there on his own

"Diana!" That's Mom calling.

but I won't tell Mom about him yet. She'll worry about the illness.

"Diana?" Her voice rises. She's wondering if I'm still out flying.

"I'm here, Mom." I close my diary and put it beside the others on the shelf.

She's sitting in the dark kitchen. The wind dropped at nightfall. Now it's calm outside. Owls call to each other in the bush. When I put on the light, Mom doesn't look at me but I can see she's been crying again, perhaps for a long time, most of the afternoon.

"It's nearly nine. Shall I do the clocks?"

"If you like." She shrugs as if it's not important, but it is. Winding the clocks in the evening is one of the ceremonies I remember from as far back as I can remember anything. Nine o'clock: wind the clocks, mark the day off the calendar; nine-thirty: contact the other settlements on the radio. It's been months since there's been any reply from the other settlements. But still we try every night.

There are three clocks. One of them is small and can be folded away inside a case that forms a stand for it while it's open. There is a larger clock in a metal frame, and the third is even larger and set in polished wood carved into fern leaves and long-tailed birds. There's an engraved silver square beneath the six on the clock that reads: *Presented to J. H. Redfern, Ph.D., President, International Society of Ornithologists, 1978– 1981.* That was my father's father. I wind the clocks in turn, starting with the smallest. They each tell exactly the same time: two minutes past nine.

"Is Dad asleep?" I ask.

Mom nods. "He'll be awake soon. We'll have something to eat when he wakes up."

The three clocks sit side by side on the windowsill. I used to play with them when I was little, putting the folding clock in the middle between the big clocks. Baby clock, mother clock, father clock. Or they were really, I suppose, Diana-clock, Mommy-clock, and Daddy-clock. Diana-clock would run along the windowsill and nearly fall off. "Watch out, Diana-clock!" Daddy-clock would

5

shout, waving his hands. "You'll hurt yourself!" "Come back here right away, you naughty little Diana-clock," Mommy-clock would scold. Diana-clock would cry and Mommy-clock and Daddy-clock would fold her away in bed till she learned to be good again.

Mom gets up and goes through the passage to the bathroom. I can hear her blowing her nose and splashing water on her face. I put some rice on to cook and start cutting up carrots and parsnips and onions, and I can hear low voices, which mean that Dad has woken up.

Mom and Dad. I still call them that even though they're not like the moms and dads in the dozens of kids' books Mom took from the library before I was born, before everything happened. They *were* like those sort of moms and dads when I was little, right up to Dad's accident, in fact. But now I think they should call *me* Mom and Dad. MominDad. I think they'd give up and wait to die if I wasn't here. They'd never remember to wind the clocks or cross off the day or make the new calendar for the next year.

Nine-twenty-nine. I rinse the vegetables, dry my hands, and go to the radio set.

Nine-thirty's the time for me to start calling the other settlements. I tune in to the first frequency. "Come in, Grey University," I say. "Redfern Lake calling. Over." Silence. I wait and try again, over and over until nine-thirty-five when it's time to switch to Eastern Works's frequency. All the settlements have special times to call each other. At nine-forty I try Crow Refinery; at nine-forty-five St. Francis General

Hospital; nine-fifty King Country; nine-fifty-five Great Western—there's no one else calling. We're the only ones. I'm getting no reply.

Mom is standing at the doorway. "Give up," she says. "It's no use and you're driving your father insane."

I make the ten o'clock call to Northern Manufacturing, although the far north settlements were the first to stop replying. I don't try the rest.

The rice is ready. I put the vegetables on top of it to cook in its steam. Mom is still at the doorway, looking out the window at the blackness. The owls have stopped. I can hear only the hiss from the stove and a soft rhythm of clicks and tocks from the three clocks. "There's no one else out there," she says, and goes back to Dad's room.

I get out plates and forks to prepare Dad's tray. He rarely gets out of bed these days. The morning he helped me fix up the wingset was the last time he got dressed.

I think about my mind making the story of my day and interweaving it with my history. I realize that I do this all the time, shaping the words about things as they're happening, getting them ready to put in my diary tomorrow. It's all I do, really. Write in my diary and watch the weather, waiting for the right lift in the wind for my wings.

There's nobody else here, Mom said. I wonder if I should tell her about that boy. No, not yet.

There's a little face outside the window giving a soundless *mew* from a pink mouth. I let Matilda in

7

quietly, gather her up, and push my face into her black fur. I hope she doesn't purr too loudly or mew for her rice. Dad will not tolerate cats.

HECTOR

I have consulted a book on astronomy in our library. I remember being taught these things when I was younger, but I never really understood them: The earth spins in a procession of planets curling around the sun. The light from the sun strikes the earth in a regular pattern, bringing light and darkness. I understand now why sometimes the light is less strong when I go outside. How strange it is to think of people once living in a world where the air endlessly changes from light to darkness, darkness to light.

Today I have come outside too soon. I can do nothing but hold my hands over my eyes. It is too painful to look at the light. I know now that if I wait, eventually the light will dim. I lie facedown and cradle my head in my arms.

I do not mind waiting. The air is cool and fresh and I can feel the strange movement in it brushing against my ears and fingers and ruffling the hair on the back of my neck. The first time I was outside I thought this soft push against my skin was caused by invisible creatures running on me—perhaps even the ghosts of long-dead things. Now I have found out that it is something more mysterious. It is called the wind.

I breathe in the outside air, deep breaths one after another, until my skin tingles. When my nose and lungs are free of the underground air, I can detect the sweet, strong, wholly unknown smells. The roaring in my ears slowly dies away and is replaced by the rustling sounds and the different songs of the birds and a far-off sighing, which is soothing and peaceful. I am rested and refreshed and more *alive* than ever before.

I hear something close to my head—but this is not a new sound. It is Stewart, my dog, waiting for me to get up and start moving. He is nearly blind and the light does not worry him. He too loves our secret visits to the outside. Bassets are noble and truly intelligent dogs, someone told me once. Stewart's my dog from the last litter and he is the best. Without Stewart I would never have found the outside. He found the way and led me through the maze to the outside world all by his nosepower.

He is almost deaf, too. I am sure *he* does not hear the sudden and close crack of branches that makes me jerk up my head. It is the smell of the huge stranded bird in the tree that starts him off barking. I did not need his excited *woo-woo-woo* with his snout in the air to guide me. I can see it. My beautiful bird has landed.

It is not a bird at all. It is only a girl, all brown and red, struggling in the middle of a lot of sticks and plastic sheeting.

Staring up becomes unbearably painful and I bend over, crumpling my fingers into my eyesockets. There are exploding white lights behind my eyes and after each explosion there's the silhouette of the bird-girl in the branches.

"Get that dog away from me!" I hear. It is a sharp voice and very loud. I have never heard anyone shout like that. It must have penetrated even Stewart's ears. His baying becomes frenzied.

It's like a nightmare. I am paralyzed by the pain in my eyes and Stewart would not hear me even if I could get myself enough under control to calm him. All I can do is rock backward and forward, holding my eyes, waiting for the explosions to stop.

I hear more cracks of breaking branches. There's a grunt, then the sharp voice says *ouch*. It's so loud, it seems to echo. Why does she yell like that? Then there's a soft thump. Stewart becomes timid and stops barking. I feel him near me, a rumbling growl in his throat, a tentative threat.

The explosions stop. There is just a mottled gray in my eyes now. I dare to open them. There she is, standing under the tree staring up. Blue and green covering her. Black hair. Light shining along a brown jawline.

The bird part of her, that which I had seen as a huge bird in the sky, is still in the tree. One wingtip is caught on the edge of a high branch and the rest has tipped over sideways through the other branches.

She is still standing there, staring upward. Now she is climbing the tree again, hauling herself up through the lower branches. Stewart stands at the foot of the tree, snuffling upward, whimpering and yelping.

The great wings do not seem to be broken, but imprisoned like those of a giant insect caught in a cobweb. She will have to release them, bring them down to the open ground, fold them around her, then burst into flight again.

She does not look human up there in the tree. I have never seen anyone so strong. She stretches and pulls with her hands onto higher branches and there she is, climbing toward the sky. She reaches the branch that has trapped the wingtip. She looks down. The whole structure, I can tell, could come crashing down to the ground when she releases it. She needs someone underneath the tree, to hold the lower wing, to steady it and help to lower it gently. She looks over at me.

I stand up. The sky is dimming. I can see things without feeling pain. I take a couple of steps forward.

"No! Keep away!" She is right. I stop. "And keep that dog away!"

Stewart is transfixed by the new scents and turmoil above him in the tree. I thump on the ground with my open hands. That is how we call the dogs. They can sense the vibrations in the hollow stone tunnels, I suppose. It works even up here. Stewart comes to me, trustingly, tongue lolling out of the side of his jowls. I hold onto the folds of skin around his neck, hauling him with me, and step back a short distance to watch.

It is amazing. She releases the wingtip from the branch, but manages to keep hold of it. She starts climbing down, sliding her grip on the wing as she moves downward, but always keeping the structure free from being caught in the branches again. She moves so surely. She's like a super-being, her physical self developed in the wilds, a perfect animal. The illness must have gotten her mind, not her body. She probably cannot read or write, or think beyond the necessities of self-preservation. As I think this, she is on the ground again, arms above her head supporting her magnificent wings.

"Go away!" she shouts, and my ears ring.

I drag Stewart to the tiny concealed entrance, and we go down into the darkness and safety of the caves.

DIANA

I have to walk home, dragging my folded wingset through the bush. The distance that I can skim over in my wings takes forever on foot. But I can't get airborne: The wind dropped as the sky darkened, and anyway there's no place in this valley between the slopes of the mountain and home to get a lift from the wind.

The moon's rising. The cold white light helps me to find my way, but it doesn't penetrate the shadows of the bush. I think I see strange shapes among the trees. A sudden owl's call makes my heart thump. I'm not used to being frightened by the dark. Tonight I feel a long way from home.

The first hour's walk is hard work, fighting through the bush and along the riverbed, trying to protect my wingset, which is too heavy for me to carry. It's all very well for Dad to say that it's far more manageable than the wingset he had when he was my age. He told me he had something called a hang glider, an ugly stiff structure which would work only if he jumped off a cliff or the side of a mountain. He said it was worthwhile, even so, because for long minutes he could imagine what it was like to be a bird. Poor Dad. He's still crazy about birds.

The bush dwindles. I'm on the slopes of the old farmland. I push through the tendrils shooting out from the patches of blackberry and cut across to the remains of a roadway. I know that long ago people drove themselves in cars along this road, following the coast for a trip around the mountain. Now the center is broken and rough with banks of blackberry leaning inward from each side. I keep to the center of the road and don't look at the shadows beside me.

I have no idea what time it is. I've never had a watch. Mom and Dad both had watches that ran on tiny batteries. When the batteries ran down, the watches were of no use anymore. I've seen Mom's watch. It has a black face with no numbers and two delicate gold hands fixed forever at twenty-five past twelve. Dad's watch is smashed. When it stopped, he threw it on the concrete outside the kitchen and jumped on it because, of course, he couldn't get more batteries. Mom told me about it. It happened when I was a baby.

I'm home at last. I look at the clocks—it's nearly eleven. I wind them all quickly. It's too late to use the radio. It's the first day ever we haven't tried to contact the other settlements. I know Mom hasn't tried.

Mom doesn't notice how late it is, but she's worried about my torn jeans and the cuts on my hands and feet. Matilda waits until Mom has left the kitchen before she hops up onto the window ledge. She knows better than to let Mom see her. There's nothing cooked to eat tonight. Matilda and I have some of the cold rice left from yesterday. I cross off today on the calendar. I go to my room and write my story for the last twenty-four hours.

I flew closer to the mountain because I could see him standing in a little clearing near the ranges. There was a dog with him I hadn't seen before. The boy was spread on his stomach holding his head. I thought perhaps he was dead and went closer to see. I caught one wing on the only big tree anywhere around—my harness hooked itself on a branch and I was stuck.

The dog went berserk down on the ground. The boy wasn't dead. He looked up and I could see that his skin was so pale, it seemed to shine in the last of the sun falling into the clearing. He was wearing a funny-looking dress like a shroud and I thought perhaps he was nearly dead with the illness and he'd been left there to die. Perhaps the dog had it too and they'd been abandoned together. The dog was trying to get up the tree. It had yellow staring eyes.

I told the boy to get the dog away. I didn't think I'd said it loudly enough to drown out the dog's noise but the boy obviously heard even in the state he was in because I saw him flinch. Anyway the dog took no notice, just carried on more. The boy crumpled up and hid his face, rocking backward and forward.

I couldn't see what state the wingset was in so I undid the harness and climbed down the tree. The wingtip was wedged on a high branch but the whole thing seemed to be undamaged. The dog, I noticed, had moved back nervously. I was worried about walking where the sick dog had been prancing around, and got back up the tree as soon as I could. It was an easy tree to climb.

I was worried that the wingset might drop too suddenly to the ground, which would really damage it. The pale boy was looking up and I considered getting him to steady it for me. After all, he was the reason I'd gotten into this mess. I'd come here only to have another look at him.

But he was so white, so weird, so obviously sick that I lost my nerve. I got my wings down on my own. He'd disappeared by the time I got down and he'd taken that dog with him.

It's a nice clearing, soft moss covering its rocky surface. If the winds were right, I could land there and climb a little way up the slope to the west to get the wind-lift for the homeward flight.

Now I wish I'd talked to him. We could have shouted at each other, not gotten too close. He's probably dead by now, and I might never find out if there's anyone else with him.

HECTOR

I climb up through the maze to the clearing in the morning. It is just before the sun has arrived and I can see everything painlessly. The sky is pink. Everything around me is wet: the ferns, the leaves, the twigs and moss and dead leaves under my feet. Stewart is excited, going as fast as he can on his short legs. Perhaps he can smell rabbits. He is never allowed anywhere near the rabbits we keep underground. He should not even know what a rabbit is.

There is a patch of grass near the clearing and Stewart is away, rushing toward four small animals grazing on the grass. I think that they really are rabbits. They look like skinny versions of the ones we have underground. Three of them race away but the fourth seems stricken and hops in a circle and does not follow the others until Stewart is almost on top of it. Stewart crashes into the undergrowth after them. There must be some memory in his brain handed down intact through five or six dog generations.

The girl has gone and taken her wings with her. I wish I had stayed last night to see her put them on and sail up into the sky. Stewart's excited barking is getting fainter. I look up at the tree at the side of the clearing. Its lowest branch is level with my head. I hold it with both hands and remember how easily she floated up through the branches. I do not know even how to start climbing a tree.

The colors of the sky are changing slowly as the light becomes stronger. There is no wind today. It is as if the world is holding still, ready for the arrival of the sun. I feel that I have seen this world before, but if so it can only have been during my dreams.

There is a piece of vivid blue on the ground near the tree. I pick it up. It is the size of the palm of my hand, silky and so light that it flutters and drifts off my hand in my breath as I peer at it. I grab it again. It is a fragment from the girl's wings.

Just then the sun breaks over the top of the bush and into the clearing. Already it is blinding and I must get back. It can only get worse. I shall have to find Stewart. I thump the ground but he does not come back. The sun is sending long splinters of light into my eyes.

He could stay away for hours. The sun cannot worry his near-blind eyes. I shall have to go back right now or I shall be missed from morning study—but I cannot find my way through the maze without Stewart.

I manage to crawl into the dimness of the cave, which marks the start of the maze. I feel tired suddenly. I usually sleep for several hours longer than I did today, like most of the rest of us; only the cooks get up so early. I doze a little and then wake suddenly. Still no Stewart. Perhaps he has fallen down a cliff. I do not suppose a blind dog would be able to *smell* a cliff, especially not with a nose full of rabbit scent. He might never come back.

I wonder how long it will be before someone notices I have gone, that I am not in the library, not in my room, not down by the animal cages, not in the water gardens, not in the kitchens or with the doctor or in the pharmacy or in the laboratory, not anywhere at all. Gone. Lost in the maze, they will think. Nobody will be brave enough to venture into the maze to find me. The other bassets would not be able to get through the maze like Stewart did. He was the only one in the last two litters with any life in him. The rest laze around and eat all day like the older dogs.

I dread my fate if separated from my underground world. I cannot survive away from it.

Then suddenly here is Stewart. He is exhausted, panting, staggering; but he is very happy.

I am saved. But I tell him that he is going to have to be on some sort of leash when we go out again. We shall probably get back safely and unseen now, but I will not go through this worry another time.

DIANA

There's a scrap of fabric torn from my wingset. I'm trying to think how to mend it. It'll have to be mended before I go up again or the whole wing will tear away. I tried to ask Dad about it earlier this morning but he's not making sense. He's dreaming away again.

I stop writing and watch Mom outside, thinning a row of carrots. She's working fast with angry energy as she always does when Dad has a particularly bad day. I watch her stand, look up and down the row with her hands on her hips, then brush her eyes with the back of her hand before kneeling again. I get up and drift around the house, searching for something to mend my wing.

HECTOR

Stewart's paws swell up and the pads under them are cracked and sore. He must have chased the rabbit for a long time. I have to hide him in my room. I would never be able to explain how his feet got into that state. I manage to get some antiseptic cream for him. I tell them I have scratched myself and fortunately nobody asks how.

It is much more difficult to find something to tie around his neck for when we go out again. It is not usual for anybody to ask for anything. We are given everything that we need. I decide to say I want a piece of cord to try to teach Stewart some tricks. I thought he would hate being led by his neck, but he seems to take it for granted.

Two days go by before we go out again. The sun has not quite disappeared. Suddenly everything is happening at once. Stewart takes off. He is unaware that I cannot see properly and he drags me along stumbling over roots and rocks and bashing into branches. He is leading *me* and that is not what I intended.

Then I hear that huge voice—"Get out of the way, you stupid idiot"—and a gigantic *whoosh* with a blast of air nearly taking my head off. It is that girl in her wings.

I risk the light to glance up and she is there, turning on one bright wing in a graceful curve to come back over the clearing. She comes down to land very gently, until the last moment when she hits the ground and she's all arms and legs and stiff unyielding wings. She unbuckles the harness that holds her to the wings, her eyes on me all the time. She is about twenty paces away. I am hanging onto Stewart, who is quieter but longing to get closer to her. Still watching me she touches one of the wingtips, which has an orange patch against the blue of the rest of the fabric. She has replaced the torn patch I found under the tree.

Then she stands by the wings and we stare at each other for a couple of minutes perhaps. Stewart is quiet now. He is squirming with his legs in the air, scratching his back on the sticks and dry leaves on the ground.

"Who are you?" she shouts. This girl always shouts.

"I'm Hector."

"What? What did you say?"

I fill my lungs with air, cup my hands around my mouth, and send my voice through the funnel straight to her head. "Hector."

"Hector? What a name." She looks as if she's going to laugh. "Well, what are you doing here?"

"I live here."

"What was that?"

This is hopeless. I send my voice down the funnel of my hands again. "I—live—here." She takes some steps toward me. Stewart gets to his feet. "No!" I say. "Stay away!"

She stops. There's a pause. "Are you—are you ill?" she yells.

"Ill? Of course I'm not ill!"

I am amazed at the question. She looks puzzled, and I realize it is not because she has not heard me. (She seems to be able to hear what I am saying now. Perhaps the illness has made her deaf. She might have come closer so she could lip-read.) No. She's looking puzzled because she does not believe me. She is looking skeptical.

"I—am—not—ill," I repeat. But I am nervous. I might be ill after talking to her. One of the little bush flies might land on her and then come and sit on me. Or on Stewart. I squat down and put my arm around Stewart. "Do not come any closer," I warn her.

"Don't worry, I won't." She pauses. "What do you mean you live here? Where?"

I hesitate. "Around here." I cannot risk saying too much.

"How many of you are there?"

"One hundred and two," I say before I can stop myself. Still it is probably a good idea to tell her the truth. She will not try to follow me if she knows there are so many of us.

Suddenly she smiles. Her angry red and brown face relaxes and I see white teeth, her head tilting to one side. "You're out of your mind," she says. She is laughing at me. I am crouching, my arm still encircling Stewart. There is a stone near my foot. I want to throw it at her. I have never felt this sort of anger before.

She looks around at the sky. She puts her forefinger in her mouth and holds it up above her head. I cringe, imagining the bugs drifting from it toward me in the breeze. "Get out of the way," she bellows. "I've got to go before the wind drops."

She is buckling on her wings. I pull Stewart with me back over the rise and we crouch behind some bushes. I cannot see her until the last moment when she is running fast up the slope, making one big push off the ground, the wings taking the last of the breeze and lifting her in a big, lazy circle over the trees and curving across the bush toward the farmland. I watch until she is a feather far below, hovering above the bush to the north, and I know she will not be able to get back and follow me underground.

DIANA

I think he's insane. All alone with that dog, he's filled his life with 102 people.

"Diana! Come quickly!"

It sounds urgent. I stop writing. It's Dad, writhing and moaning, sometimes grabbing Mom's arm and sometimes flinging her away. I've seen it all before. He wants more morphine. The blankets are in a heap on the floor and I can see his poor twisted leg that Mom and I didn't know how to set straight. I remember Mom saying "It's the best we can do. He's lucky to be alive." Looking at him now I wonder if he'd have been better off dead under that tractor.

As usual Mom wants me to dissolve some aspirin and pour it into him while she tries to hold him. Aspirin. It's pathetic. It's all we've got left. They left us enough morphine for a century's worth of pain. Dad took it all in six months and now there's none left. On some days he has triple, quadruple doses of aspirin several times over, but it's as if we're feeding him water. I've never directly asked Mom what we'll do when we use up all the aspirin. It's so sad. About once every few weeks he used to ask us to wheel him in his chair down to the blind by the lake where he watched the birdlife and made notes for his book. For months now he hasn't been to the lake. I think he finally gave up when we lost contact with the other settlements.

I try to get him to drink. His face twists and half the solution soaks into his shirt and runs down on the pillow. His eyes focus on mine, and I don't know what he can read there. He closes his eyes and becomes calm. His muscles are relaxed and he's sleeping or near sleeping in a kind of peace. Mom and I don't look at each other. We replace the covers, smooth the bed.

Mom is cooking the meal tonight. She's chopping up some of the tiny carrots she thinned out today. They're very sweet. She won't cook them, but will mix them with the hot beans and melt cheese over it all. I have time to write some more before I do the clocks.

I landed in the clearing this afternoon—nervously because I thought I might find the pale boy and his dog dead

I've never seen a dead body.

but the clearing was empty. Some birds were around, and a few rabbits, which scattered when I landed. The last minutes of the sun before it sank behind the ranges lit the edge of the clearing. Before I explored I thought I'd try a takeoff from the clearing. If I couldn't manage to get airborne, it would be better to start walking now rather than leave the long walk home till nearly dark. And just as I took off again, there was the pale boy popping up over the rise. I nearly kicked his head in.

He's alive, all right. He had that dog with him, but this time it was on a leash. He was hanging onto the leash with all his strength because the dog was determined to get away. They must be strong, those dogs like barrels on four short stalks. But then it might just be that the pale boy is so feeble.

I landed again to have another look at him—from a distance of course.

He's even uglier than I thought. He's so white, pasty, and clumsy. His eyes are puffy and red and he keeps them squinted nearly shut as if it hurts to open them. His voice is hardly more than a whisper.

He says he lives somewhere around there. I wish I could find out more about him, like which settlement he's come from and what happened to the rest of his settlement. But his mind's obviously been affected by the illness. A hundred and two people! No settlement had more than eight people. I suppose he's the last one left from a settlement that got the illness, and he's just wandering. He must have walked until he became too weak to go farther than the clearing near the mountain. Well, that's the only explanation I can think of. But I wish I knew more.

HECTOR

I have never had to hide anything before. I have never had anything to hide before.

One side of my room is the rock wall of one of the main tunnels. I have a bed and a desk and a chair. There is a pale woven mat covering the rock floor. Folded on the end of my bed is a clean tunic to wear tomorrow, left by one of the caretakers. There is no safe little spot to hide something. The room is cleaned out completely every day.

There is nothing as colorful as the little scrap of fabric in the room. There used to be a painting in bright oils on the wall facing the end of the bed. It was taken away shortly after I was moved to this room from the children's quarters. They said it was disturbing me. I can hardly remember it now. I think it was a pattern of bright yellow and red, with a black silhouette of a human figure at the bottom of the painting.

So in this colorless room the blue patch of fabric from the wing has a shocking brilliance. I realize I was very stupid to bring it with me here, even to touch it.

I consider putting it in the trash but I know the garbage sorters would find it. It is so immediately noticeable, different. There is nothing like it here, noth-

25

ing with that color or that texture. If it is found, they will know I got it from the outside. They will blame Stewart because they will know I could not have found the outside without his help.

As if he knows I am thinking about him, Stewart snuffles into my room. He hoists himself onto the mattress, turns around a couple of times, and settles down. His nose is pointing toward me, his tongue lolling happily out of the side of his jowls. He is looking sleek and fit.

I decide I shall not try to keep the blue patch, even though it reminds me of the freedom and the danger and the freshness and the light of the outside. I shall take it with me tomorrow and leave it up there where I found it. They might take Stewart away from me, to stop him leading me through the maze. I shall get rid of the evidence tomorrow.

DIANA

I've been to the clearing two days running now and that boy hasn't been there. Perhaps he's moved on (or died). I've been farther into the ranges to the northwest of the mountain, and looked all around from as close to the ground as I dare fly, but there's no sign of any settlement, not even a hut, and certainly no sign of 102 people! I thought I was lost because I couldn't locate the river at first. It's dried up so much over the last month that it looks like a ravine of smooth gray stones from the air.

I'm disappointed, I think, that the boy has disappeared.

It's time to do the clocks. Mom's cutting up vegetables for dinner. I wind the little clock and the middle clock, but the key has disappeared for the big carved clock. Usually the key is underneath it, and I open the glass door covering the face of the clock and put the key into a little hole near the center of the face. But this time the key's gone.

"Mom, have you seen the key for the wooden clock?"

She doesn't look at me, keeps on chopping. "I've taken it," she says. "Don't worry about winding that one anymore."

"You don't want me to wind it? Why not?"

"It's your father." She's still not looking at me. "He says the ticking's driving him crazy. During the night when he can't sleep, I suppose."

"Well I could take it to my bedroom or put it in one of the sheds." She doesn't reply. "Mom? We can't just let it run down. What if one of the other clocks stops? We'd only have one clock left then, and—"

"Diana. Think about it. What does it matter what time it is anymore? It doesn't make any difference."

"We have to radio the other settlements exactly on time. We *have* to know what the time is."

"There's nobody at those settlements anymore. You know that as well as I do. It's just your stubbornness that makes you keep on trying. We're all alone, can't you understand that?"

She's looking at me now. She looks exhausted, her

Well, anyway, the dog came very close to me but I was too near the ground to take off again and get away from him. It's not that I'm frightened of the dog, it's that I'd rather not get too close. He was wearing an improvised collar with a leash trailing behind on the ground, so I supposed the boy was around somewhere. I remembered the boy's name, and called out "Hector," and then the dog became very excited. He pranced around with those peculiar yellow eyes staring at me. I unbuckled my wingset and walked across the clearing a little way, calling "Hector" again.

The dog got quiet, turned, and ran ahead of me. I decided if Hector could hear me calling, he must be hiding and not want to talk to me. There didn't seem to be any point in waiting around. I started back to my wings and then the dog barked again. I watched him making little short runs, a few steps toward me and a few steps away again, and finally it sunk into my brain that he wanted me to follow him.

The dog led me only as far as the rock face rising straight up at one side of the clearing and then stood there, waiting for me to catch up. I was telling the dog that I wasn't going to try climbing that cliff when he disappeared. Vanished into the rock. I could hear him though, his oo-ooo echoing.

I found the narrow gap in the rock he'd vanished into. It was near my feet and I had to get down and wriggle in head first. It seemed to grow into a small cave inside. I could see the yellow eyes of the waiting dog reflecting the tiny amount of light that got in from outside. I couldn't see anything else. Beyond the dog's eyes it was pitch-black.

"Are you in there, Hector?" My voice boomed in the cave. The dog's eyes disappeared and reappeared several times and I knew he wanted me to follow even further. "Look, dog," I said, "there's no chance of me going into that black hole. I'm not crazy, you know. I wouldn't be able to see a thing." It wasn't that I thought the dog could understand me; I was enjoying listening to my voice. It sounded bigger and stronger.

I stood up in the sunshine again, rubbed the gravel off my jeans, and walked back to the wingset. As I got ready to take off, the dog appeared again by the rock. He sat there, his head drooping so that his long soft ears swung against the ground.

When I got home I put the flashlight on the recharger. I might go back to the clearing later this afternoon and see what the cave looks like by flashlight. It's probably a crazy thing to do. If that boy's lying there ill, there's nothing I can do to help. I keep getting a picture in my mind of that dejected dog.

It's not a cave at all. It's a narrow tunnel. I see the glowing eyes of the waiting dog. I tell it to keep away and I wriggle in. My flashlight waves around on the rough rock walls.

The dog's leading me again. I grab his trailing leash and follow. I think the dog's impatience must be affecting my brain because I don't give a thought to the stupid thing I'm doing, not at first anyway. But we seem to go on and downward for ages, twisting and turning, taking some left and right turnoffs and ignoring others. I know I'll never be able to find my way back alone. It's pitch-dark, warmish and damp. There's a smell like rotten eggs. I start to dread what I'm going to find. But I have to continue onward. The dog won't take me out of the tunnels until I've found whatever he wants me to find.

We seem to have come to an end. There's a wall of rocks in front of us. The dog starts snuffling and whining.

I suppose Hector is buried under the rocks. Now I'm really frightened. The roof of the tunnel must have fallen in and trapped him. It could subside further at any time. I shine the flashlight around. The circle of light wobbles because my hand is shaking like the rest of me. I don't want to die under a pile of rocks.

Then I hear something. It's Hector's whispery voice. "Stewart? I'm here, Stewie."

"Who's Stewart? It's not Stewart. It's me," I say. There's a silence. At least he's alive.

"Stewart is the basset. The dog," I hear. "And please do not shout."

"I'm not shouting—what do you mean don't shout! Your stupid dog's brought me through these awful tunnels and all you can say is don't shout!"

There's another silence after my voice stops ringing.

"All right," I hear at last. "I mean please talk more quietly. I do not want them to find you."

"*Them?*"

"Do you think you can get me out of here?"

"How?"

"I'm trapped on this side. But I think you might be able to pull away the rocks from your side."

"Are you hurt?"

"Hurt? No, of course not. Please hurry. And try to be quiet."

I flick the flashlight over the wall in front of me again. The rocks aren't that big, but there are a lot of them. I rest the flashlight on the ground and start shifting the rocks, piling them up on the walls on each side.

It takes a long time. It's tiring work in this steamy heat. But then finally I see the boy. He's not squashed under the rocks at all. He's standing on the other side of them. What's more extraordinary is that he's behind a sort of cage. It's a big frame of chicken wire wedged between some rocks on his side and it had been held in place by the rocks I've dismantled. Now it's easy to push aside. The dog falls over with the joy of being with Hector again. Hector and I stand face to face.

"Keep away," I warn him, remembering suddenly. But there doesn't seem much point. After all, we've been breathing the same air for several moments now.

PART
2

HECTOR

It will be daylight soon. She has left me in a place she calls a blind.

In some ways it is not so different from my room underground. There is a bed, a table, and a chair.

Nothing else is the same. There are windows all around. Outside is the dark and creaking bush.

I am on the bed. I cannot move. There is pain all over my body and inside my head as well. I wish I could fall asleep and forget this awful thing I have done.

I have run away from the community. I suppose I cannot ever go back. I do not want to think about it.

I followed her blindly through the night without considering the consequences. When she found me by dismantling the wall in the tunnel, I was so angry and shocked at what they had done that when she said come with me, I did not argue.

I followed her for ages through the bush and over rocks and stones and along hard roads through jungles of spiky plants, putting all my energy into keeping up and ignoring the pain in my feet and back and every-where all over me; and most of all ignoring the pain of being away from my underground, my safe secure place where never before has anything gone wrong. Now I know I made a terribly wrong decision.

The sky is brighter now. There is a vast stretch of water outside the blind, reflecting silvery light. There are birds, it seems like hundreds of them, swooping past the blind and plunging into the water, standing in groups in the shallows, and all of them chattering and singing and calling to one another. Stewart hears them and twitches in his sleep but does not wake. In a very short time the light will be too strong for me to be able to see anything at all.

They found out that Stewart was leading me through the tunnels to the outside world. They found the blue fabric and suspected something, so they followed me the next time I left. I was stopped before I reached the outside and taken back. They were kind and understanding. The Counselor talked to me for over two hours, while four of the others forced Stewart into the maze and built a barricade with rocks and sealed it from the inside. They used wire mesh stretched on a frame that was wedged securely between the piled-up rocks outside and rocks jutting out from the roof and walls of the tunnels.

They left Stewart outside to starve. We are people of peace. We would never kill any living thing except for food or in compassion. The whole idea of our community is to keep life safe. But still that is what happened to Stewart. This is what I could not understand. Poor blind Stewart. I wonder if he would have learned to catch a rabbit before he starved or if he would have ever found water. He stood on the other side of the barricade, his barking echoing through the maze, waiting for me to set things right. I could not break through the barricade on my own. I am not strong enough.

Stewart has been my dog for two years now. He attached himself to me from the time he was a puppy—as if he had been born for me. Nobody minded that he went everywhere with me, and I took him for granted, I suppose.

So I was not prepared for the sadness I felt about not having him with me anymore. I sat on the other side of the barricade, leaning against the chicken wire, trying to console him, and all the time thinking how he could not survive out there. So when that girl came groping through the rocks and pulled aside the wire barricade, I did not say to her, as I know now I should have, just take Stewart with you and look after him. At the time it was me and Stewart against the rest of them down there, and when she said come on, I went with her without a second thought. Now seems to be the time for second thoughts.

I am not sure if I shall ever be able to go back underground. They might not have me back. They will think I have caught the illness. Perhaps I have caught it by now. If I went back I might take it with me and then everyone down there would die.

He's just a dog, an animal that likes to be with me all the time, that's what I would have thought about Stewart. Then they tried to take him away from me. Now because of him I am stuck in this world where I cannot even see for most of the time and where I shall surely get sick very soon.

Stewart whimpers and tries to get up. Then the door to the blind opens and more light crashes in. There is someone outlined against the glare. Stewart's tail thumps on the floor. "You're okay?" I hear. It is the girl. "Poor Stewart," she says, kneeling beside him and gently touching his paws. Stewart gives a self-pitying moan and thumps his tail on the floor again. I watch her touch him, but it's too late now to worry about her infecting him. I remember during the endless walk through the darkness, the stage when Stewart fell down exhausted. She dropped her folded wings and picked him up. For nearly an hour she carried him, his hindquarters cradled in her arms, his front legs over her shoulder, while he seemed to peer past her ear to watch me staggering behind them.

It is getting more difficult for me to see. I hear her open a cupboard near the door. She goes outside to get water, I suppose, because soon I hear the tinkle of water in a tin bowl and her voice speaking soothing words to Stewart. "I've bathed his poor feet and put on some cream," she says. "Try and keep him still for a while, and you must keep him quiet."

"He is no more likely to go anywhere than I am," I say. Stewart and I are both prisoners here. She's gone again, then returns. "I've got fresh water for you," she says. "Your feet are a worse mess than his." I dimly see her holding a bowl and cloth toward me but then I have to clench my eyes shut as waves of pain from the light hit. "Just leave the stuff here," I say. "I shall do it later." She's hesitating. "Please," I repeat, "just leave the bowl on the floor."

"All right. There's antiseptic cream beside it. Look, I'll try and find you some sunglasses, okay? They might help protect your eyes from the sun."

I have no idea what sunglasses are. I say nothing. She seems to be trying to help.

"I'm going to collect my wingset. Remember, I left it by the road last night? But please be very quiet. Keep the door shut. *No one* must know you're here."

I hear the door shut and I am left with the sounds of the birds and Stewart's heavy sleep.

DIANA

I needed more sleep this morning but I thought I should get the wingset before the day became too hot.

What on earth am I going to do with that boy and that dog?

Another night when I didn't try the radio. Mom will think I'm coming to my senses. But she might not even have noticed I wasn't home last night. I saw her this morning in the vegetable gardens, and I called out that I was going to sleep for a little longer. She didn't look up from her hoeing. She's becoming very withdrawn these days. It worries me to miss the radio calls. I shiver when I think last night might have been the very time someone was trying to get through to us.

I'll have to take him food, and food for the dog—what will the dog eat? We haven't got any meat or bones. I'll have to get them both away from here before Mom finds out about him. But it's probably too late now. Perhaps he has brought the illness here already.

I had to bring him with me. It was the obvious thing to do at the time. I felt I was rescuing him—setting him free from those horrible caves and bringing him back here where he'd be safe by the lake.

I haven't asked him anything yet. This morning I couldn't ask him questions. He was curled up in the blind, huddled in the blanket and blinking like a frightened animal, white as death. His very defenselessness made me feel shy. It seemed wrong to question him. I nearly found myself bathing his hurt feet like I did Stewart's, but I stopped myself in time.

There are so many questions. Why can't he bear the light? Why is his skin so spongy-looking and pale? Why does he speak so strangely and in that whispery voice? Why has he fallen apart physically after just a three-hour walk?

Most of all, I want to know who trapped him in the tunnel. He didn't put himself there, that's for sure. Somewhere over there, lurking in the bush by the mountain, there are other people. There must be.

I'll have to take him some clothes. He must have some of his own, but who knows where he's left them? Anyway, he can't continue on through the bush and blackberry with that thin dress on, and the soft things he was wearing on his feet fell apart in half an hour last night. I can't imagine how he has survived so long.

HECTOR

She comes back late in the afternoon. I have slept away the hours of sunshine and now the shadows are growing in the little room. I lie on the bed with the blanket around me, watching the colors in the sky change and listening to the mysterious noises. There is so much life out there. Birds and insects and perhaps many other creatures I do not recognize yet; they seem to be singing and shouting to greet the gathering night.

She taps on the door and opens it slowly. She is holding something in her arms. "I've brought you some clothes," she says. "Your—your dress thing's all ripped."

"My dress thing? Oh. You mean my tunic." She brings a smell of earth and flowers with her into the room.

"Here are jeans and a T-shirt and some sneakers. I hope they'll fit you."

The clothes look like the ones she is wearing. The unusual leggings she calls jeans feel rough and unpleasant. The shoes are blue and dark red and made of fabric and rubber. One of them has two red socks tucked inside it.

"I've got some things ready for you to eat, but I'll

have to go back for them." She goes out and then looks back in. "There's a toilet just around the side of the blind," she says, and then she has gone.

I try standing up. My feet hurt when they hit the floor, but no more than the rest of me. Every muscle is aching. I inch over to the door and open it, and for a moment I sway there looking at the lake. It takes me ages to get outside. Stewart watches every painful movement and I tell him to sit quietly.

I try on the jeans and I suppose they fit, but I would not know. I have never worn such things before. They are very uncomfortable. I think about putting my tunic back on but she was right—it is torn right up one side. The T-shirt is made of a softer fabric than the jeans and it feels more pleasant against my skin.

I smell the food she is bringing before I hear or see her. She comes in with two bowls and a cloth bag.

"Do the jeans fit?" she asks.

I am bending down, inching the socks over my damaged feet. "I think so," I say. "They feel strange." I stand carefully, concealing the pain.

"They're not bad. A bit big perhaps. Will they do?"

"Yes." My mind is really on what she has brought to eat. I am starving. Stewart is looking excited and drooling. He lifts himself to a sitting position. She hands me one of the bowls and the bag.

"There are potatoes with rosemary and tomatoes. You'll find a spoon and a fork in the bag, and there's fruit in there for you too." She holds out the other bowl for me to look into. "I brought this for Stewart. I hope he'll like it. It's rice with some dried fish in it.

41

I really don't know what dogs eat. Except bones, of course, and we haven't got any of them."

"He will like it," I say. I find the spoon and start eating. She puts the bowl in front of Stewart. He eats it in two great gulps then noses the bowl over to see if there is any more underneath.

While I am eating I notice her eyes on the tunic that I dropped on the floor when I changed clothes. The blanket from the bed is on the floor beside it and my feet are resting on that. I know nothing about this world away from underground, so I do not know if there will be caretakers to come every day to fix up my room and bring me clean tunics. There is something about the way she is eyeing my discarded tunic that makes me uneasy. Perhaps there are rules here about used clothes that I do not understand yet.

"Should I get Stewart some water?" she asks. "Would you like some? It's not from the lake. There's a rainwater tank outside." I nod and she takes Stewart's bowl and a cup from the bag. While she is outside getting the water, I pick up the blanket and my tunic and fold them, and they are neatly on the end of the bed when she returns.

"We're very short of water just now. Many of our tanks are empty. *Surely* it'll rain soon. I hope so. The gardens are drying up and we haven't dared to try using the water in the lake. Well, we haven't had to. There's always been plenty of rainwater before."

"What do you mean, you have not dared using the water in the lake?"

"Well, because of the poison of course." She's sitting in the open doorway looking out over the lake. The poison?

She goes on: "This lake's always looked like this, lots of birds and frogs living here. Dad's always said it didn't get affected by the poison, but all the same, we've never risked using its water."

There are so many questions. I do not know where to start asking. There is the big first question, and before that is asked and answered the others cannot be asked. That is the question about the illness.

"It is a very beautiful lake," I say. I can see it shimmering silver beyond her. Somehow I am sure it is beautiful, even though I have never seen any other lake.

"There's a story about this lake. It happened a long time ago when there were lots of people living here. Oh, not right *here* of course. It was always empty and peaceful here. But when there were lots of people living in cities and towns and things. Well, anyway, there was this guy living in the city and going to work every day in the rush hour and then fighting his way through the crowds at lunchtime and waiting in lines to get on the bus at night back to his apartment building, which was full of the sound of screaming kids and fighting couples and televisions and rock music and pneumatic drills from road workers doing overtime. At last he couldn't stand the noise any longer—he could never get the peace of silence in the city—so he came here."

I do not stop her, although she is talking about things I cannot understand. I want her to keep going. Nobody has ever told me a story before.

"He just took off and ended up here by this lake. He stood here and looked at the water and the bush, which had never been touched, and started to think, This place has always looked like this—I could be standing here at any time in history. He liked this idea and he tried to think about it but the noise was so huge—the frogs were roaring and the birds in great flocks were shrieking around his head. He held his head and screamed because he could never get away from the noise to the silence he craved. He thought, This is it. I've had enough, and he lay down and put his head under the water in the lake because he'd decided to drown himself. He waited, then under the water he could see that the lake had become a bright clear red and that all around him were faces of people, dogs, cats, radios, factories, and birds and fishes and frogs with mouths opening and shutting, and that the noise was worse than he'd ever heard before. He sat up and wiped the water off his face and out of his eyes. Everything was silent. He looked around. The birds were still swooping. The wind still fluttered the bul-rushes. But he could not hear any of it. He was quite, quite deaf." She stops.

"That is the story?" I ask her. She nods. "Is it true?"

"Probably not."

"So it was not someone you know?"

"Of course not," she says scornfully.

We are both silent for a moment.

"I drank some water out of the lake last night," I say at last. "So did Stewart. After you left us here."

It is too dark for me to see her face, but I can see

44

the sudden stillness of her shape against the light on the lake.

"If you get sick from poison in the lake," she says in a low voice, "you know we can't look after you. We don't have any medicine." She stands up quickly, and then she is gone.

DIANA

I leave him and his dog in the blind. It's quite dark by now and I stumble on the trail from the lake. There's a little *mew* and I scoop up my black cat Matilda into my arms. She purrs and nuzzles into my neck. How can anyone be so stupid as to drink water out of a lake? Where's he been all his life that he doesn't even know that much?

I take some more rice from the bowl in the kitchen for Matilda. Mom's sitting in the next room, watching the dark window. If she has noticed that I've taken food from the kitchen, she doesn't mention it.

"Do you want me to get something ready for you and Dad to eat, Mom?" I call to her. She doesn't answer, and at first I think she hasn't heard me. But then she turns her face toward me and I'm shocked. Perhaps I haven't looked at her properly for ages. She looks haggard, about a hundred years older than she should be. "Mom," I say, going over to her, "what's the matter? What's wrong?"

She covers her face with her hands, and I put my arm around her shoulders, awkwardly, because it's a long time since I've hugged her.

45

"It's pointless," she says. "It's just *pointless* going on living like this."

"Living like what?"

"You don't know what it's like for me—" she puts her hands down and looks at me. "No, you poor child, you really don't know what it's like, do you? I keep forgetting. You've never known anything different. You've lived like this all your life." Her shoulders sag and she looks again at the window. I feel dismissed, useless to help her.

I remember a time long ago, years before Dad's accident, when Mom was in tears and Dad was trying to comfort her much as I am now. It was different then because Mom wasn't broken and defeated. She was in a rage. "How much longer?" she was shouting. "How much longer do I have to put up with this? Stuck here in the bush by a duck pond—no television, no newspapers, no one to talk to, no new books, five minutes each night talking to people stuck in some other bit of godforsaken bush with nothing more to tell me than how many stupid carrots they've planted—" Dad was able to comfort her as I am not because he missed all those things too. I was six or seven then, and I said "Tell me about television and newspapers," because I knew there'd be wonderful stories for me as they almost fell over themselves telling me about things they'd seen on television, old movies, plays, series, news stories about disasters and political scandals written in the newspapers and shown on television almost as soon as they happened. Then there'd be the stories about the lake and the people who used to live here. And they'd be laughing and happy again and talking to each other more than to me. They'd open one of the precious bottles of wine to drink and I would be given a tiny drop mixed with water and it would be pink and sour and lovely—now I realize that this sequence of events occurred perhaps many times while I was little. After I was nine or ten nobody talked about newspapers or television anymore. I still read about them from time to time in the books that are stacked around the house, as well as reading about train trips and holidays at the beach and people falling in love and kids going to school and lots of other things that don't happen anymore.

"Mom, why don't you have a rest tomorrow? A day off."

"A day off to do what?" she asks me coldly. "To go to the movies? Out for lunch at a restaurant? Go and see a play perhaps?"

"To have a rest. At least have a rest from the outside work. I'll do the milking and the chickens in the morning, okay?" She still stares at the dark outside the window. "Why not, Mom? You could do some sewing. You used to like sewing."

"What do you suggest I sew? Curtains to stop the neighbors from looking in?"

"You could make me a dress."

"A dress!" At least she smiles. "You—in a dress?"

"Yeah. I could put it on in the evenings and we could play chess." That's the wrong thing to say. Dad and Mom used to play chess often, right up until he started to disintegrate. They were fiercely competitive about chess. She has tried to teach me but my brain refuses to take in the rules. Now she has no chess partner.

"I'm joking, Mom. I don't really want a dress." She doesn't reply. "But, anyway, I'll do the early morning stuff tomorrow, okay? You sleep in, promise?"

A couple of hours later I wind the two clocks. I try the radio, calling each settlement. Then I go to bed, but I slept this afternoon so I'm not tired. I get out the diary.

He looks more normal in jeans, but still so frail and white. It's not that he looks ill exactly. He's like a plant that has tried to grow in the grain shed in the dark. Pallid leaves that should be green and glossy. Perhaps, after all, that's all the illness does to you. If so, it wouldn't be all that bad. On the other hand he might be in the early stages. Perhaps he hasn't got it at all.

And then the idiot goes and drinks the lake water. If he gets sick from the lake poison on top of everything else, I can't expect him to leave soon. He simply won't be able to. I don't know how much longer I can keep him a secret from Mom. She's depressed and unhappy now. It would be the last straw for her to find out there's someone sick actually living here among us at the lake. I should never have gotten into all of this.

I still haven't asked him anything, and he's told me nothing and asked me nothing. I'd have thought he'd have explained something about how he got trapped in those caves, but not a word. He's pretty mysterious. I was looking at his dress tonight—the light was shining in the doorway and it showed up a deep row of embroidery around the neck and at the end of the sleeves. The dress is made of soft pale material like a fine woven wool, and the embroidery's in a glossy thread of the same color, and it was this glossiness that shone in the light. But I think he didn't like me looking at the dress, because while I went out to get some drinking water he hid it under the rug.

HECTOR

Stewart is getting restless. While it is still twilight and I am able to see—in fact, I can see very well in this half-light, it is what I am used to—I find a coil of thin rope among many other interesting things in the tin cupboard. I decide to come back to the cupboard soon, but in the meantime I tie one end of the rope to Stewart's collar and the other end to a leg of the bed. I prop the door open. He has the illusion of freedom. He can limp in and out, snuffle among the grasses outside the blind near the lake, but not wander too far away.

One side of the cupboard is full of stacked papers: notebooks and loose sheets covered in fine writing in black ink. It is too dark for me to read it. There are heavier things in the other side. I identify a hammer and a knife and another cup by touch, because by now there is no light at all. Away from home I find I am unable to see anything for most of the time. Underground the tunnel lamps glow all day and all night.

Then I find the candles. There is a whole box of them. I can smell the wax and feel their smoothness. Beside them a small box, which clatters when I shake it. Matches.

I love the smell of candles burning. Years ago we used them underground for a while when there was trouble with the generator. Lighting this candle now and fixing it upright in a cup brings back the underground and everything else I have not wanted to think about. The candle lights up the room and throws my reflection on the glass of the three big windows. I look at this unknown me in strange clothes. Stewart sniffs at the candle smell. It is new to him. He was not born when we needed candles underground.

With the candle I explore the cupboard further. I am looking for a book or something else to read. I have to settle for the handwritten papers. It is a diary of some kind, only not as interesting. It is more like a record in painstaking detail of every single thing that every single bird on this lake did, day by day. There is a book for every two months or so and the first starts in August 2008. Over seventeen years ago.

I flick through some of the books. The entries are spare, scientific, almost coded, and there is little that makes much sense to me.

There is a difference in the last book. It is dated June 2024. There have been very few entries since 2022. There is only one paragraph:

The experiment can be called a success. The test birds have settled and there are now eighteen fine specimens covering several generations showing every sign of successful pair-bonding and nesting. I can consider my work regarding their care to be completed. I am no longer necessary to their survival. Perhaps I never was. After all, it's no secret that their existence is contingent upon the absence of humans with their cats and dogs and guns and other toys. Soon the beauty of the birds will have disappeared and only the birds themselves will remain here, undisturbed forever, because only humans name things "beautiful" and it is only humans that destroy the things they call beautiful

Here the last entry stopped, the writing large and wobbly and so different from the first entry in 2008, with its firm, small lettering:

Blind established at D9 and equipped. Test birds due tomorrow. Temp. 10°C, no rainfall, wind light NW.

I find a large map falling apart along its folds, clearly a plan of the lake and the land around it, divided up into a fine grid. The vertical lines are given letters and the horizontals numbers. I find the blind marked at the axis of D9. Other positions on the map are marked with small crosses and words like "nested 8.2.09," and I find these match up with entries in the diaries, like "nest found B12." Slowly the code-like entries start to make a little sense.

Stewart comes inside with a kind of urgency about him that startles me. He folds himself under my chair, his nose pointing to the open door. He is making smothered growls. Then I can hear it too. It is the sound of hesitant footsteps coming toward the blind.

It cannot be the girl. Stewart does not growl at her. I am unable to see anything through the huge black windows, just a reflection of me with staring eyes.

There is suddenly a woman standing at the door. She is half-lit by the candlelight. She is older than the girl, but not much bigger. She is holding a black shawl around her with a long fringe that reaches to her heels at the back. Some of my fear goes when I see how alarmed she is.

The silence goes on and on, except for the sound of Stewart's growls, which are becoming hysterical. I bend down to grasp Stewart's collar to try to calm him. As I move, she comes a step closer and I can see that she is holding a small revolver and that it is pointing at me through the fringe of her shawl. Now my fear returns.

When she speaks, her voice sounds harsh and loud like the girl's did when I first heard her. "Who are you?" Her eyes are wide and look shocked.

Now Stewart does bark, but it is a strangled sound and I realize that in my fear I am holding his collar too tightly. But his noise makes the woman step back and I see the gun is now pointing at Stewart. I keep hold of his collar and stroke his head and shoulders with my other hand to calm him. "He is harmless," I manage to say. "He would not hurt anybody. He is just surprised to see you."

"*He's* surprised to see *me*? That's amusing," she says. She is not looking amused. "Well, why are you here? Who are you?"

"I needed to rest because my feet were injured. So were Stewart's."

"Stewart?" Her eyes look for someone else.

"Stewart is the basset," I explain. "I am Hector." I do not know what else I should tell her. I know the girl would not want me to say that she brought me here.

"You shouldn't be here," she says, "touching my husband's books."

"I was looking for something to read."

We are still staring at each other. She has the same black eyebrows and dark eyes as the girl, but her hair is long and almost white. I notice that the revolver is no longer pointing at us.

"Where are you from? Where are the rest of you?"

"I've been walking a long way. I am on my own now."

"But what settlement are you from?" She is firing questions and I am not used to inventing untrue answers.

"A settlement south of here—"

"Which one? What happened to the rest of you?"

When I do not answer she stops asking. After a time she speaks again and her voice is more gentle. "All dead no doubt from the illness, and you left alone."

Then she adds bitterly, "And you have to come and bring it here to us."

"I do not have the illness," I say firmly.

"How can you be so sure," she says. "You look sick. So thin and white."

"I am *certain*—unless of course I have caught the illness since I have been here."

"There is no illness here!"

We are staring at each other again, both hostile. I am wondering if she is telling me the truth. Probably she is wondering if I am telling her the truth. I want to believe her. It will mean that the girl is unaffected too. The woman does not believe me, I can tell. Her eyes are moving over me, and they stop and look at my arms. I see my arms are covered with little red lumps that start to sting and itch as soon as I become aware of them.

"You don't have to leave immediately, now that you're here, if your feet are injured. But you shouldn't have the door open. You're being eaten alive by mosquitoes."

"There are mosquitoes here?"

"Look." She points at the ceiling. I can see groups of tiny slender insects, some flying. "Can't you hear them?"

I have been hearing a high-pitched droning. But there are so many new sounds. "So those are mosquitoes?" I ask.

She looks puzzled. "You can't tell me you've never seen mosquitoes before," she says. "They've been flourishing ever since it happened. Where have you been all your life—living in a hole in the ground?" I look at her closely—perhaps the girl has said something to her already? But she goes right on talking and I do not think she meant anything personal by a hole in the ground. "You'll probably find a mosquito coil in the cupboard. It's green stuff in a sort of spiral. You light it with a match and it smolders. That'll get rid of them. All you have to do is be able to stand the smell."

She's turning to go. "And keep that dog quiet and under control," she adds.

"He is harmless. He is blind and would not hurt anything."

"I've always been scared of dogs," she says. "I was almost glad when they were the first to go when it happened. I never thought I'd have to see another dog ever again." She looks back at Stewart, suspicious. "How come that dog survived?"

I do not know how to answer her. She goes away, closing the door.

I hug Stewart. There are two more things I have learned about this life away from underground. There are mosquitoes and there are no dogs. "Poor Stewart," I tell him. "It looks like you will be the last of a fine breed."

DIANA

Early this morning I took some fresh milk to the blind and found the boy sitting outside wearing only jeans and with his long fair hair darkened with water.

55

He said he'd been for a swim in the lake. I was horrified but I suppose he has to wash somewhere. He was wearing the sunglasses I'd taken to him last night with the fruit. It was quite different to see him not cringing away from the light. He seemed like a stranger all over again.

I spent all today working in the vegetable gardens, watering them. Carting buckets of water from the pond below the waterwheel. The water pressure has fallen too low to be able to use the hoses. It must rain soon.

I haven't seen much of Mom today. I think she must have been resting and reading as I suggested. I saw her carrying a pile of books during the morning.

I haven't seen much of the boy today either. Too busy with the watering. Good excuse. The longer I put off asking him questions about himself the harder it gets to start. I feel awkward with him. I wonder how long he'll stay here.

<u>HECTOR</u>

Slowly I am becoming accustomed to this strange world. I am no longer apprehensive about the new smells and sounds or amazed at the endless variety of birds. I like the feel of the wind pushing my hair around and the warm sun on my arms. But I'm starting to feel restless. I want to know more about it all.

I envy the unknown bird-watcher his knowledge which gave him hours of informed observation. To my uneducated eye they are just birds. Different colors and shapes of course, some flying, others swimming or wading in the swamp. I wish I knew more about them. I wonder why there are no books about birds in the underground library.

I am slightly hungry all the time. Stewart is very hungry all the time.

I have walked right around the lake. I used the trail marked on the map I found to get through the swamp. I did not find any of the nests marked. Most of them are too far off the trail to be visible and I did not want to risk leaving it. I led Stewart by the cord attached to his collar. Both of us walked very slowly—me trying to get used to the curious rubber shoes rubbing against my painful feet—but even so, it whiled away only an hour or so of the long day.

My unoccupied mind turns many times to the underground. I miss its peace and security and the calm routines that occupy each entire day. I am uneasy here. Sometimes I feel overwhelmed by the openness and the strength of the light.

The woman comes back while I am sitting in the doorway of the blind and wondering about home. She is wearing jeans like mine but cut off above her knees. She stops a short distance away and puts a pile of books on the ground. "I brought these for you to read," she says. "And something for you to eat." She leans a small basket against the books. "I don't know what you like. What sort of books, I mean. Heaven knows as far as food goes there's not much choice." She's looking at me carefully. "Does the sun bother you?"

she asks. She comes one step closer. "My husband used to wear sunglasses very much like those." She is talking about the glasses with dark lenses the girl brought me. It is true; they do protect my eyes from the daylight. The girl was right.

The woman sits cross-legged on the trail, facing me. "I'm sorry if I was abrupt last night," she goes on. "It was seeing the candlelight in the blind that startled me. It looked exactly as it did when Evan worked here. I could see it from the house, a glow away through the bush. Seeing it again last night made me very nervous, but I had to come and see what it was." She glances over her shoulder back along the trail. "You can't see the house from here in the daytime or the blind from the house, but at night that little candle glow reaches the house. It's so black and empty outside at night. Evan worked here during the nighttime often. I'd be with Diana when she was a baby, and I could see that tiny light from the house windows."

Stewart is moving toward the woman as she speaks, but I am keeping a firm hold on his leash.

"And of course," she continues, "when I saw you, I was worried—they said we had to be so careful about people wandering in the bush. Some people escaped, you see, when they were already sick, and some didn't leave when all the others did and even if they weren't sick then, they soon would be without treated water and so on. You know all this anyway. But you'd be too young to remember it, of course. What are you, fifteen, sixteen? I thought so. Much the same age as Diana."

58

Diana. Perhaps that is the girl's name and this is her mother. Unless there are still more of them here.

"There's a rainwater tank behind the blind," she says, "which will be safe for drinking. At least I hope there's some water there. We're very short of water. You know how it hasn't rained for ten weeks."

I don't know. I am not even sure what rain is. Of course I do not tell her this. "There's some water in the tank," I tell her.

"How are your feet coming along? Getting better?" She is asking me how much longer I am going to stay. "Still a little tender. But they are coming right."

She reads my mind. "It's just I don't know how long the tank water will hold out."

"It's all right. I am using very little of it." Perhaps they are depending on it in case their other supplies run out. "I am not washing in it. I washed myself in the lake."

"In the *lake*?" Her face has the same shocked look as the girl's had. "It's extremely dangerous, you know." She points across the lake over toward the rock face falling straight into the water. "It's deep in the center, very deep. It falls away suddenly like an abyss hidden under the surface."

"I did not go in very far."

"There's a story about that lake. Shall I tell you the story?" She's still looking toward its center. "A fisherman came here once—a very fine fisherman with all the best fishing gear. Nets, waders, a selection of the finest fishing rods, a case of handmade flies for trout fishing, top quality hooks, and all the rest of it. He'd fished in every famous spot in the world and caught all kinds of fish. He'd won a prize in the Bay of Islands for making a kingfish he'd hooked fight on the end of his line for the longest time on record. He boasted there was no type of fish in the world he hadn't killed at least one of." She looks at me. "Shall I go on? Do you want to hear the story?"

"Of course," I say.

"Anyway he found this lake and thought he'd try his luck here. He'd never fished here before. He was half-afraid that here in this beautiful lake high up near the mountain he'd find a new type of fish and prove his own boast had been wrong.

"He waded into the shallows and cast his line out. The line sagged and he realized the sinker had gone down no distance at all—it was still shallow where it landed. He waded farther and cast again. The same thing happened. He waded out farther, the water creeping up past his knees, but he was wearing his full-length waders, and on the final step he cast his line as hard as he could. But that final step never finished because when he tried to find his footing, there was nothing there and he was falling down through the water. His huge waders filled up and dragged him down even faster as he struggled to kick his way back to the surface.

"The farther he fell, the greater the weight on top of him seemed to be. The water was darkening. Suddenly in the blackness he saw a huge diamond shape, about the side of his chest, glinting silver and hanging in the water. He threw his arms around it and hung

60

on with all his strength. Someone saw me fall in, he thought, and I'm going to be rescued.

"And indeed he was being pulled up through the water out of the darkness. He saw the edge of the crevasse he'd stepped over, then he was being dragged through the greeny shallows. As soon as he could get his head out of the water, he yelled 'Not so fast! You're hurting me!' but it didn't slow down. 'Slow down!' he yelled as he sped over the rocks. 'Not so fast!' The movement stopped and he opened his eyes. Above him he could see two gigantic waders like the trunks of two great trees. Above them a massive chest with one huge arm holding a fishing rod, the other a glinting knife. On top of it all, so high up in the sky that it hurt the man to peer up so far, a monstrous head.

"The fishing rod dropped like a pine tree being felled. A finger and a thumb zoomed down and picked the man by his feet off the sinker he was grasping, and banged his head a couple of times against a stone to stop all his noise. Then he was laid beside the rest of the catch on the shore."

She looks back toward me, looks me up and down.

"Still, you'd probably be safe. I suppose you know how to swim."

"No," I say, blinking at her story, "no, I don't really."

"You don't know how to *swim?*" She looks amazed, then frowns and smiles. "Of course. Silly of me. I keep forgetting. Diana never learned either. Nowhere to swim, is there? We never dared to try swimming in the lake, even though Evan always swore it wasn't poisoned. Well, perhaps you're being our guinea pig, Hector. How do you like that?"

I have no idea at all what she means by that.

"I'm talking too much, aren't I? Gabbling away. I haven't said so many words all at once since—I don't know when. You'll have to forgive me. It must be the shock of seeing a new face."

I do not mind her talking. It also means I do not have to talk myself.

"Your arms are getting very pink in the sun. You should take care. Do you usually wear long sleeves?" She is looking puzzled and her eyes are on my hands.

"I am glad to have the books," I say to change the subject.

"That's okay. Just a few novels. I hope you like them."

She is getting up to go.

"Do you mind telling me—what were the test birds?"

"The test birds? Oh, of course, you've looked at Evan's journal. Well there were many different sets of test birds. In the last few years before it all happened, Evan rescued hundreds of birds from their natural habitats—which of course were just being obliterated one after the other—and brought pairs of them here to see if they would adapt."

Before it all happened. That's the second time I have heard that phrase. Before what all happened? What do they mean? The woman is still talking.

". . . you'd be lucky to see them right now, especially after we've been making all this noise and you've been crashing around in the water and the dog's been here and everything. You haven't disturbed any nests, have you?"

"No, I am sure I haven't."

"Good. I'll bring you a bird manual with pictures. There's a whole shelf of bird books up at the house. Are there any other books you'd like?"

"No, not that I can think of right now." If they have one whole shelf just for bird books, they must have thousands of other books as well. I am very pleased—it is hard to ask questions straight out, but if she brings me books, I can perhaps find answers for myself.

"You wouldn't perhaps like a book on how to play chess?" she asks hesitantly.

"I know how to play chess."

"Would you like a game of chess sometime soon? Shall I bring a board with me next time?"

"I would like that very much," I say.

"Right," she says with satisfaction. Then she pauses. "I'll figure out some way we can play," she adds, and I remember she thinks I've got the illness. I feel angry that she still has this suspicion and I nearly tell her she can keep her chess—I would rather read books anyway—but she has turned and is heading away along the trail, striding like Diana does.

DIANA

"Mom, we've got to talk about the water. The pressure's so low that the hoses won't work anymore."

"I know that. I had to cart buckets of water to the chickens this morning."

"Well, I had to cart about a million buckets yesterday to put on the gardens. Look." I show her my palms. My hands have tough skin, but even so they're reddened and swollen with two deep blisters forming at the base of my thumbs.

"Poor little thing," she says teasingly, and taps my nose with her finger. I jump backward in surprise but she doesn't seem to notice, she's turned back to the sink to wash potatoes. "Well, got any ideas about the water?"

"No." I hadn't gotten as far as thinking of ways to solve the problem. She's the one who knows all about the generator and how to fix things, but because of the depressed way she's been lately I wasn't sure if she'd even noticed how low the water level was getting. Also, much of my attention at the moment is fixed on removing her from the kitchen so I can get some milk and food to take to the boy. But she seems to be cheering herself up by having a cooking binge. She's even soaking some of the precious dried mushrooms.

I turn my attention back to the water. "We could dig a trench from the pond under the waterwheel down to the gardens. Like an irrigation channel."

"You must be joking!" She looks around at me and I notice that her eyes are clear and direct again, not unfocused and dim as they have been recently. "It would take a couple of ditchdiggers with machinery a week to do a job like that. And you with your hands in that mess. You couldn't dig into a bowl of custard at the moment."

Custard. I bet she's going to make custard.

"There's the lake water—" I could cut my tongue out. What made me say that? The last thing I want is for her to start investigating the lake water with that boy hidden there.

"Diana. We can't possibly use that water. There's no way we can test that much water and so we can't be sure it's safe. Put that idea right out of your head." I needn't have worried about drawing her attention to the lake. "Look, it's bound to rain soon. We'll wake up one morning and it'll be pouring down. You'll be grumbling that you can't go up in your wings. Why don't you go up for a fly now?"

I mutter something about repairs.

"Well, why not go and fix it? What do you need?" she asks.

It's almost as if she's trying to get rid of *me.*

Just then we hear a clattering and a squeaking from the side of the house. We rush over to the window. It's Dad, painfully and slowly driving his wheelchair over the ramp from the French doors of his room down to the grass.

"Oh my God," Mom says. "It's months since he's been on that ramp. I hope it doesn't collapse under him."

He makes it to the grass and the tensed muscles in his face relax as the wheelchair rolls more easily over the dry ground. He goes as far as the row of rhododendrons.

"Mom! He must be getting better!"

"Perhaps. Look. He's got his binoculars."

Slowly he lifts the binoculars in both hands to his eyes. We can see even from here how his hands shake. After a long moment the binoculars tumble from his grasp and spill over the arm of the wheelchair to the ground. He is still for a moment. Slowly, creakingly, his head goes back and he roars out a long howl of despair.

It echoes in the still, hot bush around. Mom and I stand in shocked silence. Then I hear an answering *woo-wooo* from the direction of the lake. It mingles with the echoes of Dad's cry and continues it.

Quickly I turn on a tap to drown the noise and I fill a cup with water for Dad and hand it to Mom, thinking she *must* have heard Stewart. But she's white-faced and staring at Dad. Perhaps she was too worried about him to notice. She dashes out the kitchen door and over the grass to the wheelchair. I grab some milk and rice cakes and take off through the dining-room doors in the direction of the lake.

HECTOR

I hear a terrifying howl echoing out of the bush. It startles Stewart into replying. For ten minutes I sit still, waiting to see what it was, but everything is silent again. Even the birds seem shocked into quietness. Then the girl—Diana?—comes hurrying along the path. Stewart is sulking inside the blind under the bed. I stamped my foot in its tough new shoe when he barked and I ordered him inside. He is not used to being reprimanded, but the howl startled us both. I was reading when we heard the howl, but I see the girl coming through the bush in time to hide the book.

She brings me more milk and some flat rice biscuits. The last few times she has been here she has left immediately, as if she has better things to do, but this time she sits down beside me.

"I couldn't get here sooner. I suppose you're getting hungry."

I am not hungry, really, at all. The woman came early and brought milk and apples and a little pot of honey, which was strong and beautiful and which I ate with my finger while she sat and watched me from a distance. I am worried about having Diana sitting here in case the woman comes back again. She said she will return later with the chessboard.

I am not sure what Diana would think if she finds out that her mother has discovered me. Somehow each of them has dragged me into her plan not to tell the other. At first I thought it was a plan working to my advantage. Stewart and I will get all the food we want and more. But it is getting complicated in practice. I am not used to this sort of deception. I can guess what will happen. They will find each other out, then unite and turn against me.

I pretend to drink deeply from the milk and take a small bite from the rice biscuit. It tastes good. I find I am hungry after all.

"Where's Stewart?"

"Inside. He is in disgrace." She gets up as if to go

in, and quickly I call him. I do not want her to go into
the blind and find the rest of the books her mother
has brought me. Stewart is sneaking out from under
the bed anyway, pleased to hear Diana's voice, hoping
I will not notice.

"Poor Stewie," she says, and he gallops the last few
steps to her, wagging his tail, slobbering with delight.

"You don't have to *spit* on me, Stewart," she says.
"Let's have a look at your paws." He rolls over immediately. "Hey, does your dog talk English?" she asks
me, smiling. She must know we have not got the illness. She would not be so kind to Stewart if she did
not believe me. "They're all better, Stewie! What a
clever dog." She rubs his chest and he squirms with
pleasure. She looks up at me. "Did you leave him any
milk?"

I tip some into his bowl by the step. He scoops it
up fast with his great tongue. She holds his ears out
sideways to stop them from swinging into the milk.

"What is your name?" I say.

She waits till Stewart has finished, and releases his
ears. "Diana," she says, coming to sit down again.
"Your name is Hector, isn't it?"

"Yes. I told you. Ages ago."

"I know. I don't like it all that much."

"Well, I cannot do much about it, can I?"

"Perhaps not, but I can. I can call you something
else." She looks at me, her eyes narrowed into a stagy
deep-thought pose. "I'm not sure yet. I'll think of
something."

We are both silent for a moment.

"What was that noise I heard?" I ask her. "That howl?"

"Oh . . ." She shrugs. "That was my father. He's not well. He—he gets headaches."

"Very often? They must be bad ones."

She shrugs again. It is clear that she does not want to say any more. "What do you do all the time here?" she asks.

"I have plenty to do." But I can't tell her about reading novels. "It is taking a lot of time to get used to . . . all this." I sweep my arm around, indicating the light and the sun and the bush and the birds and the lake. "I am trying to make my feet more tough. I've walked around the lake several times."

"Great. How are your feet? Are they better?"

"Almost. These are good shoes."

"*Shoes?* They're not *shoes.*"

"What are they then?"

"Well, I suppose they are shoes, but nobody calls them that. They're sneakers, or runners, or joggers. *That's* what you should be doing. Jogging. That's supposed to make you fit."

"Jogging?"

"Like running." She gets up and runs a few steps along the trail, turns and runs back. "And you're supposed to breathe properly—oh, I don't know much about it really. I just read something about it somewhere." She sits down again. "It's a pity you can't come and help me in the food gardens. That's real hard exercise."

Now, I am telling myself, tell her now that her

mother knows about me already. But it is too late. She is going on, "You've only been here a couple of days though and already you're starting to look different. You're starting to get a suntan. Your arm's getting all golden."

"Is that from the sun?"

"Of course it is."

My arms do not look golden to me. They are a pinky yellow.

"And you can see properly now."

"Not really. Not without these glasses."

"Try it. Go on."

I take off the glasses with my eyes shut and open them slowly. She's sitting there, hands clamped over her mouth, obviously helpless with laughing.

"Your face," she says. "It looks so funny."

She spins out of focus briefly, then locks back. I can see without the glasses. We are sitting in the shade. I still cannot bear to look where the sunshine falls directly.

"You've got a bright pink face and big white circles covering your eyes!"

I put the glasses back on. The people here are very direct. I am not used to comments about my looks. Or about my name.

"Hector," she says, "have you really been living under the ground? In those caves?"

I nod.

"How long?"

"Always."

"All your *life*?"

"Yes."

"How *awful*. That horrible dark place. And your parents—what about them?"

I hesitate. "They too have always lived underground, probably."

"Probably? Don't you know?"

It is my turn to shrug and look reticent. She wouldn't understand. It is impossible to explain to her in a few words one of the basics of a whole lifestyle that I start to suspect is so very different from hers. I have no idea who my mother is or who my father is. They would not know about me either. Well I suspect my mother would know. After all, I was the last child to be born. Somewhere underground in the file center there will be a carefully kept record, but it is not considered necessary that I know the identity of my father or that of my mother.

I do not want to tell these things to this girl. She has had such a stupid and negative reaction to the notion of living underground. She does seem childish really, much more of a child than she seemed as the beautiful bird-girl. I do not think I like her much now. She probably is younger than I think, just overgrown on all this outside air and sunlight.

She stands up. "I'd better go," she says. "See you later. Bye, Stewie."

She has gone only a few seconds when Stewart becomes alert and growls gently deep in his throat. And I know, I just know that the woman's coming this way with her chessboard and the girl and the woman are going to meet each other on the trail.

DIANA

There she was, tripping along the trail toward the blind with her basket like Little Red Riding Hood. I saw her first and made sure she didn't see me by leaping in among the flax bushes. I followed her back to make sure. She was indeed going to see him. She gave a big wave as she approached the blind. They're clearly great pals.

She carried the basket balanced on a chessboard. Chess. Just the dreary sort of game he would play. And I suppose she's got his dinner there for him too. Probably the fancy stuff she was making with the mushrooms.

That's what makes me so mad. He let me go on taking him pathetic cups of milk and boring rice cakes while she's been feeding him as well.

And pretending he was filling up his time going for walks and getting fit. That's where she was going yesterday with a stack of books. While I was getting blisters.

Why couldn't he have told me? I was the one who rescued him and gave him somewhere to live. Well, he can just burrow back under the earth for all I care now.

The only good thing about him is his dog, and I like cats better anyway.

PART
3

HECTOR

The days drift past and still I have not faced the question of my future. I am not used to making decisions.

Do I decide for myself what to do next, or let someone else decide for me? If I decide for myself, it seems I have two options. I can move on from here with Stewart. Or I can return underground.

The first option is limited by the fact that I do not know what to expect to find away from here. The problem with the second option is that I think they will not have me back underground.

Letting someone else decide for me what to do amounts to nothing more than sitting around here and waiting to see what happens.

In the meantime the time passes easily. The bits of my skin that the sun gets at are developing a rosiness. I found some wire cutters in the tin cupboard and cut the legs off my jeans. Now that I can keep the mosquitoes away during the night, the itchy red lumps have gone.

Beth brings me books and we play chess. She's a better player than I am, but I can still offer her a good challenge. I can identify many of the birds now. Stewart somehow understands perfectly our dubious position here, and is quiet and well-mannered at all times.

I was wrong the day I thought Beth and Diana were going to meet on the path. Beth arrived (at that stage I didn't know her name was Beth) and I waited for her to say something. She didn't. She showed me the food she'd brought me and pointed out the mushrooms with which she was indulging me. I did not tell her that mushrooms are the most common vegetable for us underground. She had two chessboards, two sets of pieces.

"You have a board and one set of pieces," she said, "and I'll use this other board and set of pieces over here. We can tell each other the moves. Black or white?"

I have not yet been able to convince her that I have not got the illness. But then the subject has not come up since that first day.

"I've tried to teach Diana how to play chess but she doesn't seem to have the interest."

I thought at the time she was dropping Diana's name into the conversation as a kind of test for me, giving me the opportunity to admit that I know Diana myself.

"She hasn't got the powers of concentration. Always thinking about something irrelevant. Brain like a butterfly."

So it was then that I told her that it was Diana who had brought me here to the lake. She was surprised, so surprised that I had to believe she and Diana had not met each other on the trail. I told her Diana had said no one should know I was there. She said, "So that means Diana doesn't know I've found you," and I told her Diana didn't know.

Each day since, Beth has brought me more novels, always saying as she hands them over that she hopes I have not already read them. Of course I have not. These are all published in the 1980's and the 1990's and some from the early 2000's, and there are no books underground published after 1968. But I have not told her anything about underground. As for Diana, she has not been here for days.

DIANA

Mom's watching me, I can tell. I catch her looking at me and twice she has asked me if I feel okay. The little rat must have told her. She watches what I do in the kitchen, how much food I take. There's no problem since I'm certainly not going to take food or anything else to the blind or go anywhere near it until he's gone.

I wrote that over a week ago. Haven't written anything since. I'm not doing anything much except carting water to the gardens and avoiding Mom.

I leave my diary unwritten for yet another day and wander down to the grain shed. I've decided to carry on with normal life regardless of the intruder. I'm going to get out the wingset and have a fly.

The three wild cats that live in the grain shed are lolling in the sun and they scatter when I approach.

75

They're looking fat and sleek. They live on the families of mice that live on spilt rice and wheat. Dad hates cats, but he's always tolerated the grain shed cat family as long as there are enough mice to distract them from the birds. Somehow for years there's been a perfect balance. Matilda was the only kitten to survive the last litter. She sees me and gallops over. I pick her up and carry her with me to the side of the grain shed where I keep my wingset.

I haven't looked at the wingset since I dragged it home after bringing Hector back to the lake. I didn't take the time then to look at it properly, but I knew there was some damage. When I open it out now I can see that two of the struts are broken and one side of the left wing has a long rip. I can't understand why it's that bad. The damage must have happened when I was trying to help Hector and letting the wingset drag any old way along behind without taking care of what was banging against it. It will take, I don't know, *hours* to fix it and need materials I don't even know if I'll be able to find. I sit on the ground beside it and wonder where to start. Matilda winds herself around my ankles, purring.

There's a snuffling among the tree ferns, and a brown and white face appears. It's Stewart. He gallops over to me looking happy and pushes his great wet nose against my hand. Matilda has sprung away, her backbone arched into a comical question mark of dismay, eyes like saucers. She has never seen a dog before.

I had decided that I wasn't going near the blind while that boy was still there, but I'd been reckoning without Stewart. I can't let him wander around here. There are the chickens and the cows he might chase or start digging in the garden. I've read that these are the sorts of things dogs do. He's not supposed to be running loose. I stroke his long silky ears. Matilda has calmed down and started stalking Stewart's wagging tail. She's not a grown-up cat and still chases everything that moves. Hector is supposed to be keeping Stewart tied up. I decide to take Stewart back to the blind and tell Hector so right now.

I can see Mom in the distance collecting vegetables far from the trail to the blind. "Come on, Stewie," I say, and then notice his collar's missing. That's probably how he got away. It wasn't a proper dog collar anyway, just a length of braided twine tied in a knot. There's a leather belt in my room somewhere. I run up to the house to get it after telling Stewart to wait there for me. I've heard Hector tell Stewart to do that and he seems to understand. I don't know if he'll take any notice of me.

I come back with the belt and some scissors to shorten it and make more holes for the buckle. Stewart's waiting there for me, and there's Matilda disappearing down his throat. Her head's right inside his mouth. I'm about to scream and attack to save her when her head pops out again and she leaps onto his head, rolling off and having a bite of his ear on the way down. They seem to be having a game.

I get the collar fitted at last. It's hard because Matilda thinks it's part of the game. "Come on, Stewie. Wait here, Matilda." (I'll try it on her.) When we get to the trail to the blind, Matilda's still following along taking swipes at Stewart's tail. I stamp on the ground and shout, and she disappears.

There's no sign of Hector at the blind. The door's closed and I can't see in the windows, even the one that's open, because there's been some fine netting material stretched right across the windows on the inside. I can guess that mosquitoes have been getting at him, and Mom has brought him some of the shade fabric to make screens.

I see someone running around the other side of the lake. It has to be Hector, I suppose, but he's looking very different. He's wearing shorts and no T-shirt. His skin has completely lost its milky pallor and he seems to be running strongly. He disappears where the trail goes through the bush and then I see him again bounding up on top of the rock face above the lake. He stops running at the highest point and jumps heavily into the water. I hear myself gasp. If he has hurt himself, I wouldn't know how to rescue him.

There's a lot of splashing, and I can see he's moving through the water to the point where the trail comes back down to the shoreline. He gets out of the lake and shakes the water out of his hair as he comes along the trail. He seems a bit winded now, and he's slowed to a walk as he picks his way across the swamp toward the blind. His shorts, I see, are the jeans I brought him. The legs look as if they have been hacked off with a bread knife.

Stewart senses him and goes to meet him at the

edge of the swamp. Hector sees his new collar, looks over to the blind, sees me.

It's an awkward meeting. It's as if we're strangers. He's like a stranger to me for the third time. He's been away from the tunnels for about two weeks. He looks like a different person. He acts differently too, and his way of speaking has lost its stilted formality.

"Well," he says, "you found the time to drop in."

"Stewart came up to the house," I say. "You're supposed to keep him tied up."

He laughs easily, sitting on the grass outside the blind and leaning back on an elbow in one graceful movement.

"Stewart can't keep up with me anymore," he says. "I suppose he wandered off while I was running."

"You shouldn't let him," I say. "He might disturb the birds."

"The birds! They're okay, got everything they want here. One dog's not going to hurt them. They've got it made."

I look at him sprawling on the grass at the edge of the lake, squinting only slightly in the sunlight.

"Just like you, I suppose," I reply in a frosty voice. He just smiles at me. I stand up and get away from the blind as fast as I can.

HECTOR

I don't know what made Diana leave so quickly yesterday. She made Stewart a beautiful new collar, dumped him here, and took off. I was pleased to see her. I wanted her to see how I have become strong and nearly as fit as she is. I can talk to her more easily than I can to Beth. Perhaps that's because Diana knows something of where I come from.

I've started on a fitness program. Beth didn't ask any questions when I said I wanted to get fit. She brought me some books she had up at the house. There's one on sun worship and bodybuilding that I like best. There's another on training for marathons, and one on yoga and meditation, which I know something about because there are yoga classes underground. I've chosen parts from them all and put together a routine, which I follow each day. Every day I can run one more time around the lake before getting tired. Best of all, I'm not getting headaches and blinding flashes inside my eyelids at night when I'm trying to sleep. More easily each day I can stand the light.

I'm reading a book every day. I'm learning heaps about this world. Beth brings the books to me but she never takes them away again after I've read them. She doesn't take away the plates I've used, or the spoons and forks. I rinse them in the lake and leave them with all the others on the desk in the blind.

One day I'm reading a novel about whales when I hear a squeaking sound coming along the trail. Stewart tenses. The squeaking stops. I hear a man's voice sounding annoyed, then more squeaks. Around the corner of the trail, coming toward the blind, is a man in a chair with wheels at each side. He's turning the wheels with his hands, and the chair is moving toward me.

I am sitting on the grassy patch outside the blind, leaning against the doorway. The man comes right up until he's quite close to me. He looks tired and very sad. His eyes are two deep pools. He's breathing deeply as if he has expended too much energy. He takes a while to catch his breath and speak, but he does not look surprised to see me.

"You're not upsetting the birds, I hope," are his first words.

"Not at all," I say. I suppose this is Evan, Diana's father, Beth's husband. "I keep to the trail and don't touch any nests."

"What's that?" he says, looking past my knee to Stewart's face poking around it. "A dog?"

"He's very quiet," I say. "He's blind and he does what I say."

There's a long silence. He seems to have left me and gone into a reverie, watching a drift of birds on the far side of the lake.

"I've been bathing in the lake," I say tentatively, "but I'm sure it doesn't disturb the birds."

"You've been in the lake?" His attention snaps back to me. "Are you all right? No ill effects? Blisters? Hair falling out?" He looks at me closely. "No," he says, leaning back and watching the lake again. "You look quite well." His words come slowly, long spaces between the phrases. "I knew the lake wasn't poisoned. Always knew that. That's why I took the risk to stay here. It's not river water, runoff water, that's the reason. It's underground water. Springwater. Comes up from way under us."

"I'm feeling quite well, thank you."

"Good," he says.

I think his attention has gone away from me again. His right hand starts to shake and he grips it with his other hand. "You're a chess player," he says. He's looking at the board set up on the step outside the blind door. It's my latest game with Beth, still in progress, waiting till she visits next. He doesn't seem to see her board, pieces in identical places, set up over there. "I used to play a fair game myself," he continues. "But not now. My concentration's gone. I can't . . ."

He is silent for another long moment, and I can see he's still watching the calm water.

"Do you have a story about the lake?" I ask him.

"There are lots of stories about the lake. It's a lake rich in stories." He pauses again. "My best lake story is in there, in the blind, written in all those journals. But there's another story someone told me once."

I wait.

He goes on at last, his voice falling into chant-like patterns as if it's a story he has told many times before.

"There was a family living here by the lake, and they were all very happy.

"At least they all thought they were happy. But one by one the children grew up and became discontented and left to live in the city. Soon only the old couple was left here.

"The old couple overcame their sadness at losing their children and were soon as happy as before. After all, they still had the beautiful lake, which they loved very much.

"One day a real estate agent came to see them. He had a client, he said, who wanted to buy the lake and the ground around it. He intended to build a township for the executives working at the new industries near the city. He would drain the swamp and make a golf course for the executives' leisure time and build a jetty into the lake so the executives' children could race their speedboats.

"The old man said he wanted some time to think about this and invited the real estate agent to take a rowboat out on the lake while he did so. The real estate agent rowed out to the center of the lake and the old couple stood on the shore.

"Suddenly a terrible storm developed over the lake. Great black clouds gathered. Thunder rang out and there was lightning, and a solid column of rain poured down on the little rowboat. Soon the little boat filled with water and sank, taking the real estate agent with it down to the bottom of the lake, while the old couple stood in the sunshine on the shore and watched.

"The old woman said to the old man, 'McGregor, you shouldn't have done that.'

" 'It wouldn't be safe out there for children in speedboats,' said old McGregor.

"A while later a man and a woman came to see them. They were from the government, they explained. The government intended to take over the lake and the ground around it for a tourist resort. There would be motels and a high-rise hotel, and they'd drain the swamp to build a shopping complex. They'd build a ramp into the lake for waterskiing, and there'd be a floating restaurant.

"The old man said he wanted some time to think about this and invited the couple from the government to take a rowboat out on the lake while he did so. The couple from the government rowed out to the center of the lake and the old couple stood on the shore.

"When the rowboat reached the center of the lake, it started to turn around and around. The movement became faster until it was spinning. All the water was turning and forming a huge whirlpool. The little boat was rapidly sucked down to the bottom of the lake, taking the couple from the government with it. The old couple stood on the calm edge of the lake, watching.

"The old woman said to the old man, 'McGregor, you shouldn't have done that.'

" 'It wouldn't be safe out there for a floating restaurant,' said old McGregor.

"Some time after that the grown-up children of the old couple returned for a visit. 'You know, Mom and Dad,' they said, 'there's a lot of land here. We could sell it for a great deal of money and you could live out your lives in style in a place in the city. The government was interested a while ago and also an entrepreneur. We're sure we could get them interested again.'

"The old man said he wanted some time to think

about this and invited his grown-up children to take a rowboat out on the lake while he did so.

"The old woman said to the old man, 'No, McGregor.'

"But the grown-up children were keen on the idea and started rowing out. They were squealing and laughing as they had when they were little. The old couple stood on the shore and watched.

"The lake had never looked so beautiful. It was glassy smooth and a deep turquoise color. A white heron swooped upward and perched on a high branch, watching. The bush was dark and still, waiting.

"The grown-up children out on the lake grew quiet, then said to each other, 'It's so very restful and lovely here. I'd forgotten the peace and the beauty. We should let it remain like this. We can bring our children here and their friends, and then our children's children. We should make sure the lake stays like this forever, a sanctuary.' And that's what they decided.

"The old couple stood on the shore, watching. The old man saw that nothing had happened to the grown-up children on the lake. He could not know that the lake had acted upon them as surely and irrevocably as it had upon the real estate agent and the couple from the government. He thought the lake was going to be destroyed. In deep despair he turned and walked away into the swamp.

"The old woman and the grown-up children searched for a long time, but he was never found."

His voice has sunk to a whisper. His eyes have closed.

85

"I'm tired," he says. "Take me home." I don't move. I'm thinking about this. "That's the trouble with Beth," he mumbles. "Judges people on whether they can play chess or not." His eyes open. "Please, take me home," he says.

His eyes close again. I'll have to wheel him back. Well, why not? They all know about me now.

DIANA

I'm in Mom's sewing room looking through the piles of fabric in one of the chests. There's a footstep on the veranda outside and Mom comes through the French doors into the room. She sees me surrounded by fabrics. "Can I help?" she asks.

"I'm looking for some of that thin woven plastic stuff to mend the wingset."

"Wrong chest," she says. "It's in that one, I think." She points to the chest I'm sitting on.

"I've already looked in there."

"Perhaps there's none left. Will anything else do? Can it be sewn up?"

"I don't know. Probably not."

"Well, don't look so stricken. Let's have a look at the damage."

I lead her outside and over to the grain shed. The wild cats scatter as we approach. "It's a good thing Evan can't see those cats," Mom remarks.

Matilda bounds up when she sees me. I ignore her, pretend I don't know her, but she's too dumb to catch on. "Friend of yours?" Mom asks when she sees Matilda jump into my arms and nuzzle my neck. "Another one of your little secrets, Diana?"

"She's not doing any harm," I say. "She helps catch the mice." I put her on the grass, and as if to prove her worth, she attacks a butterfly.

"I don't mind your having one little kitten for a pet, Diana. What I do object to is your stashing a stranger in the blind and not telling anybody about him."

"Well, what about you?" I say loudly. "You've been feeding him for a fortnight and not telling anyone."

"Better that he has food to eat than start catching the birds or coming up to the house to steal. You brought him here, Diana, and you've probably brought the illness here as well."

"He's not sick."

"How can you know that?"

"Why don't you drive him away then? Send him and his dog on their way? You wouldn't do that, would you? It's more important for you to have a chess partner, isn't it?"

"If he stays down there at the blind and we don't get too close, I don't see what harm he'll do."

"Staying there getting fat on our food that takes us all our time to get enough for us. Yeah, I know I brought him here, but then he was a helpless, frightened . . . *alien,* almost. Now he's a self-satisfied sloth. He's having a fine old lazy time. Why can't he help with some of the work if we're going to keep on feeding him?"

"Don't shout, Diana." She looks around to make sure Dad's not in hearing distance. "He can't come up here because we don't know whether he's got the illness. We can't take the risk. And we can't risk Evan getting to know about him. Evan's just starting to get a little better. Any shock will put him right back."

"Well, how long's that boy going to stay down at the lake growing fat? Has he told you anything about himself? I bet you don't know anything about him except he plays chess."

"It's clear he comes from a settlement where everybody else has died. He has probably lost all his friends and family, Diana. It's not surprising he doesn't want to talk about it yet. He'll tell me when he feels able, I'm sure."

"None of that's true, Mom. He's just let you believe that. He's from under the *earth*. He has lived all his life in a *cave*. Like a beetle. He'd just crawled out when I found him."

"That can't be true. I don't understand why you've taken against him so much, Diana. You must have liked him enough to risk bringing him here."

I'm not sure about it all either, now. I kick at the grass. "He comes from underground. It's true."

We don't hear the squeaking wheelchair till it's quite close, and then I glance at it for only an instant before fixing my attention on Stewart and Matilda, who are attacking each other like old friends. Mom's also shocked into silence. It's Hector who is pushing the wheelchair.

I hear Dad's weak, rambly voice. "My young friend here was kind enough to bring me back."

Nobody says anything.

"Well," Dad goes on, "here we all are, then."

HECTOR

It's a big wooden house with verandas on all four sides. The rooms are large and full of light with double doors opening onto the verandas. Most of the rooms have fireplaces.

They put me in a room with a bed in it big enough for four people. There are shelves of books on one wall, and another wall is stacked with sealed cardboard cartons. "More books, mainly," Diana told me. "Mom helped herself to almost half the books in the city library once she made the decision to stay on here, you know, when it all started happening."

"We've used this room mainly for a storeroom," Beth said, "because it's sunny and dry. I hope you'll be comfortable here."

Beth and I play chess the first evening, finishing the game we started early this morning. It's strange to be using one board and be playing face-to-face with her on one end of a table in the middle of the room. Our light comes from a weak globe hanging above us. It lights only our faces and the chessboard. The rest of the room is in darkness. I can almost imagine I'm underground again, playing chess in the dim lighting, except for the night owls calling outside and the distant swishing sound of the waterwheel.

Diana comes in. She's carrying some kind of lamp,

which throws strange shadows on her face. "I'm going to try the radio," she says to Beth. She ignores me.

She takes the lamp to the radio transmitter I noticed earlier. First she winds two of the three clocks sitting on the windowsill above the radio. The biggest clock has stopped, its hands pointing to five-past-three.

Then she sits at the radio. I hear her voice speaking urgently. "Come in, Grey University, Redfern Lake calling. Over." This goes on for some time before it changes. "Come in Eastern Works. Redfern Lake calling. Over."

"You're not concentrating," Beth says to me. She has demolished my defense in a couple of moves and the game's more or less over. She's watching me watching Diana. After about half an hour Diana stops. She's silent, still sitting at the radio set.

"Perhaps you can tell Diana there's no point calling those settlements anymore, Hector," Beth says. Her voice is gentle. "Which one did you come from?"

Diana speaks from the pool of light by the radio. "Isn't it time you told Mom where you're really from?" I don't say anything. Diana goes on. "Mom's been trying to be tactful and kind because she thinks you're grieving for your lost family. I think you should tell her the truth."

I'm aware of Stewart lying under the table, his chin resting on my foot. You got me into this whole thing, I tell him silently. "I didn't mean to mislead you, Beth. I don't come from a settlement—well, not from any of those Diana was trying to contact."

Beth and Diana are watching me, each face floating

in the shadows in its own circle of light. "I come from a community quite near here."

"That can't be," Beth says. "There's never been a settlement near here. We've been the only ones here always. Well, ever since everybody went away."

"I lived underground. There's a system of underground tunnels and caves to the west of here."

"Underground?" Beth's voice sounds faint. "How many—how many of you were living there?"

"A hundred and two. A hundred and one now that I've gone."

"The rest are still all there, Mom."

"They found out that I'd discovered a way through the tunnels to the outside. Well, Stewart found it really. They didn't want me to go outside anymore. So they blocked up the tunnel."

"And left Stewart outside to starve," Diana adds.

"Then Diana found Stewart, and he led her through the maze to me, and she unblocked the tunnel and let me out."

Beth's looking at Diana as if she's never seen her properly before. "You just followed a strange dog and—"

"Oh, no, I'd seen Stewart before. And him." Diana nods toward me.

"And he told you he wanted to escape?"

They're talking as if I'm no longer here. I break in. "I *didn't* want to escape. Not really. At the time I think I was shocked at what they'd done to Stewart. It was the first time something, well, bad had happened."

"You didn't want to escape?" Diana looks amazed.

"But it must have been ghastly living down there. All dark and wet—"

"Not at all. It's very pleasant down there. I liked it." They're both staring at me again. I realize I spoke loudly. "And anyway, I'd always lived there. I didn't think about living anywhere else."

"But how could you see in that dark? Whatever did you find to eat?"

"We've got lights. We've got a generator like you have, only much bigger and better. We've got a hot-water spring as well. And we grow things and make things to eat. There's a huge kitchen with five cooks. And there's a doctor and a librarian and a huge experimental laboratory and—"

I'm getting angry. They're sitting there looking at me as if I'm something that's crawled out from under a stone. As if their lives are so much better. They've got nothing here compared to what we've got underground.

"And it's *safe*," I tell them. "Nobody's ever died underground. Ever."

DIANA

Dad insisted that Hector stay here at the house with us. He just took it for granted Hector would move in. Mom took Dad aside and I heard her hissing something about the illness. Dad's voice roared out— for a moment it lost all its usual faintness and he sounded like his old self—"Nonsense! That boy's not sick. A picture of health, aren't you, boy?" "I've never felt better in my life," Hector said. To do him credit he looked embarrassed at what was happening. But then perhaps it was because he saw his lazy life at the lake disappearing.

Mom led the way inside, Hector wheeling Dad's chair. She sent me out again to get the things from the blind. It took several trips. There was a great stack of dishes and over thirty books. On my last trip I tidied the blind, folding up the rug on the bed and putting Dad's journals back in the cupboard. I found the dress with the delicate embroidery and took that back too.

I don't know what I feel about Hector being here. It all seems to have gotten out of hand. I suppose it's got its good side. Dad seems to like him, and he appeared to be willing to learn how to help Mom look after Dad tonight. And he'll be able to help in the gardens. Having someone else to carry buckets of water has to be good.

On the other hand, things are changing around here already. Mom and Dad seem to hang on to every word he says and he calls them Beth and Evan.

I thought when Mom found out where he came from, it would put her off. But once she got over her first shock, she asked him question after question.

He told us this strange story of a man with a kind of vision of a community that would be safe. This man decided to save a chosen group of people from all the evil things that were going to happen to the world. Hector spoke about this man as if he were magic, had known in advance about the chemical pollution and the nuclear accidents. Hector said this man traveled around the country and even overseas, collecting a group of people who would join him. All sorts of people, experts in every field needed to keep a community self-sufficient. One by one these various scientists and experts disappeared from their normal lives and joined him. Doctors of medicine and science, mechanics, plumbers, artists, carpenters, dressmakers, musicians, cooks, cultivators.

Meanwhile huge preparations were being made in the secret underground system of tunnels and caverns. A power generator was set up using the network of underground springs and a radical new chemical method. Plumbing was installed, electrical wiring, heating systems, and carpentry. Endless tons of supplies were brought in. He said it all happened over half a century ago.

Mom said she couldn't believe it. She couldn't believe people would cut themselves off from society if they didn't absolutely have to. She got that look on her face that meant she was remembering her old life.

"But they were right, weren't they?" Hector said. "They're still alive. Everybody else is dead. Apart from you there's nobody left here at all."

"Oh, no," Mom said, "that's not true. They've just gone away until it's safe to come back. We were left here as guardians, sort of. But they'll be back."

"Where from?" he asked. "Where are they?"

Mom looked out the window up at the black sky. "Up there," she said. Then Hector looked at both of us very strangely.

HECTOR

I'm trudging with two buckets of water toward the largest patch of vegetable garden, where Diana waits to pour the water along the rows while I take another two buckets to fill with more water. It still hasn't rained. It seems I've stepped above ground into a spell of drought longer than anyone remembers. It's hot. The water sloshes pleasantly on my bare legs as I walk.

"You're wasting it," Diana says as I approach her.

"Not really. It feels nice. And most of it's falling onto the spinach."

"The spinach is really suffering from the dryness. Look at the leaves. They're like leather. No new leaves growing."

I sit down between the rows and watch her. "Diana, this is crazy, carrying water like this. There must be an easier way to water the gardens."

She glances at me but carries on working. "Sure there must be. Got any ideas?"

"What about the lake? Plenty of water there."

"We can't use the lake. I told you. We don't know if it's safe. If it's poisoned, then the poison will get into the plants and then into us."

"I don't believe the lake's poisoned. Stewart and I've been swimming in it every day for ages. And," I add, "drinking it."

"Oh, no. Tell me you're joking."

"The water tank by the blind ran out after I'd been there a couple of days. I didn't have much choice. Anyway, I couldn't stop Stewart from drinking the lake water."

Stewart is lolling in the shade a few yards away. He hears his name and lifts his head. He's been following me with the buckets, fooling with the water as it splashes out, but his strength ran down after my tenth or eleventh trip. Diana finishes the watering and sits down in the next row.

I go on: "Anyway, what's so perfect about the water we're using from the waterwheel pond?"

"That's springwater, underground water. It's always been safe."

"I think the lake's safe too. Evan says that's underground water."

"Probably, but such a big expanse of water—there's bound to be some ground seepage. That's why we've always been careful . . . anyway, seeing you're clearly not poisoned by the lake water, perhaps . . . but even if we could use the lake water, we've still got to get it here."

The soil we've just watered is already drying in the hot air. She sifts it absently in her fingers as she talks. "I tried to talk to Mom about digging irrigation trenches from the stream, but you know her. Blind faith the rain'll come tomorrow. She says the day we start a huge project like that it'll start pouring."

"It might almost be worth tempting fate by starting then. We've got this saying underground: If you don't want it to rain, take an umbrella with you."

Diana laughs. "That's mad. None of you have seen rain for decades."

"I've never seen rain."

She leans back, shading her face and looking up into the blank blue sky. "It can be boring, the rain. Sometimes it rains for days on end here, especially in the winter. But right now some rain would be fantastic."

She is relaxed and generous with smiles today. It's unpredictable. It's something I've noticed in the days I've been living at the house with this family, this unpredictability of moods, the tensions that are liable to flare up without warning. It's generally between Beth and Diana. Sometimes each of them seems to be seeking an alliance with me against the other. Less often I find them allied against me. Sometimes I feel I'm living one of the novels I've been reading whenever I get the chance. This kind of emotional politics is new and disconcerting for me. Even now I can't relax and take Diana's sunny mood on its surface value. I find myself wondering if she's been arguing with Beth.

Diana scatters a handful of dusty earth. "We're not even keeping up. The ground's as dry as it was when we started this morning."

I look across the sheltered grove of vegetable plots, fringed by the bush on the far side, and by a row of rhododendron trees on top of a rise on this side. Beyond the rhododendrons is the house. Farther beyond that is the trail to the lake.

"If we could get the lake water as far as the rhododendrons," I say, "we'd be all right."

"But how do we do that? It's a long way to the lake. We'd be digging forever."

"We mightn't have to dig. Why not a tube of some kind running across the top of the ground?" I have a picture in my mind from somewhere but I don't know the words I want.

"PVC tubing!" crows Diana. "Of course! Come on. We'll go to the wonder shed."

"Wonder shed?" Stewart sees us going and struggles to his feet to follow. Diana's little cat appears, stretching. I try to keep up with Diana's strides across the rows, up the slope to the rhododendrons.

The little black cat is a revelation to me. I've never seen a cat before. That sinuous softness with hidden spikes. Much less inviting are the large motionless cows and the two monstrous bulls. I'm not interested in seeing any of them again.

"It's the big shed with the generator. It's called the wonder shed because, well, it's Dad's story really. I wasn't even born then." She's still ahead of me. I thought I was getting fit. "The story is, after they finally agreed to let Dad stay on here to continue his bird project and so on, they brought out all the things they thought he and Mom would need to live here on their own. At first Dad kept records of what was brought and where it was stored, all the food and clothes and farming equipment and fuel and medical supplies—and so on—as it went into the grain shed and the house. Then people had to start leaving and some of them got the illness and it all got chaotic. Dad started bringing truckfuls of supplies himself and he dumped them in the generator shed. There's heaps of things in there we've never investigated. It's all last-minute stuff they thought we might need sometime, or that Dad grabbed on the final trips before it was too dangerous to go to the city anymore."

"Diana," I say, "how long did they think you'd be staying here alone?"

I don't think she hears me. "So now if we want anything, someone says try the wonder shed. We don't always find what we're looking for, but we usually find something interesting. A new kind of seed, dried soup, things like that. A year ago we found a carton with packets of coffee beans in it. Mom nearly went crazy with joy."

I catch up with her at the rhododendrons. She's waiting for me. "I suppose they thought we'd be here for as long as it takes. As long as it takes to become safe again to come back."

I ask the same question I've asked before. "Where are they all, then?"

"I don't know," she says, walking on, not looking at me. "Somewhere safe. Waiting."

"Diana, it's not true. Everybody else has died. Finished. Everywhere. There's nobody hanging about waiting to come back."

"That's not true, Hector. *They're coming back,* that's what's true."

"How do you know it's true?" She doesn't answer. She plods along a pace or two in front of me. "You can't prove it's true, can you? It's just what your parents said. You're only believing that because it's what you've been told."

She stops and turns to face me so suddenly, I nearly bang into her. "Yes," she says, her face screwing up, "it's what Mom and Dad *told* me. And they *know*. They lived through it all. Where was all your group during that time? Hiding under the ground somewhere. No idea at all about what was going on."

She walks on. I hurry after. "Some people came to see us once, underground. It was years ago, before I was born. They said everyone was dying. They said the cities were wiped out already. They said the very land itself was infected and all the water, and that the poison was spreading in the sea and coming in along the coastlines. They said the whole world was dying."

"What happened to those people?"

"I don't know."

"Did you ever talk to them yourself?"

"I told you, I wasn't born then."

"So you don't know either. You just believe what *you've* been told."

"But it makes sense, doesn't it?"

"I suppose it does, to you," she says. We've reached the generator shed, and she looks back at me as she pushes the door open. "It's what you've believed all your life. You've never known any different. Like you'd never seen sunlight or birds and you probably still don't believe in rain."

She goes inside. I do know, in fact, what happened to the people who stumbled accidentally on the old cave entrance and came underground. I don't know how long they had been wandering, becoming sicker. They can't have been part of the organized settlements Beth has told me about. They waited outside the locked gates, bloated with the illness, their skin purpling and blistered. They were in pain and had trouble shouting their pleas to the Counselor, who stood well inside the tunnels to keep safe. The Counselor threw some food and painkillers out to them. They died very soon. Immediately the Counselor arranged for the old entrance to be dynamited, and the bodies were buried as the entrance became blocked by huge piles of rubble.

DIANA

We found plenty of PVC tubing in the shed. I knew all along it was there, stacked along the length of the shed behind piles of cartons and lengths of timber. I've seen it other times I've been scavenging in the shed, but I pretended to be surprised to be in keeping with the wonder shed story. Really, of course, I know every detail of the things in that shed.

We started pulling the tubing out of the shed and stacked it outside. We found boxes of gadgets to connect the pipes and make them go around corners if we want. I felt optimistic about the whole project and refused to think anymore about Hector's latest story.

Mom came over with drinks of iced lemon. She said it would never work. "Sure," she said, "the lake's on higher ground than this, but it's sitting in its own basin. You'll have to get the water over the edge of the lake basin before it'll run down the pipe."

I reminded her about siphoning the last inch of gasoline out of the last drum for the tractor years ago. I went on talking quickly because I saw immediately I shouldn't have reminded her of that day. I said that perhaps the same principle would work with the lake. Mom looked skeptical. Hector was saying "Gasoline? Tractor?" I have to explain so many things to him.

By sunset tonight we'd laid the pipes end-to-end nearly half the distance to the lake, and dragged more of the pipes out ready to start again first thing in the morning. During the afternoon when it was really hot, Hector persuaded me to go for a dip with him in the lake. At first I said I'd just watch him. Then Mom arrived and went into the water herself, and enticed me in, and she gave us both our first swimming lesson!

HECTOR

Beth doesn't want to play chess tonight. Instead she leads me into her sewing room, as she calls it. She shows me inside the tall cupboards that line one wall. They are full of clothes, all new. There are stacks of jeans like the ones Diana brought me the first day I was here. There are rows of shirts on hangers, some made of thin material, some thick, and there are piles of woolen sweaters in bright colors. "There are plenty of clothes here," Beth says. "You're sure to find things to fit you. There are things in every size. Just take what you want."

I'm looking at the complicated sewing machine standing on a table by the window. "I hardly ever use that," Beth says. "There are so many clothes in the cupboard, it seems pointless to make more."

Beside the sewing machine, standing in the corner, is a baby's crib. It's full of neatly folded baby clothes and brightly colored toys. "That was Diana's," Beth says. "I should put it all away into a storeroom. It's not as if I'm going to have any more babies." She picks up a soft stuffed animal with round ears, its fur worn off in patches. "I wanted to have lots of children. But I didn't count on what it would be like giving birth without doctors and nurses to help. Diana was born over the radio, you know." She smiles as she tweaks the animal's ear. "What a performance that was. Evan running around doing the best he could, getting instructions over the radio from a woman at the St. Francis settlement. Me screaming my head off in the background. I decided I'd never go through it again. It took a fair while to get over the birth. For a long time it was touch and go for Diana."

She becomes quiet and puts the toy back with the others. Finally she says, "Evan wants to see you. Why don't you go to him now?"

Evan's room is filled with the rich light of the sunset. I think he's asleep but his eyes open as I hesitate by the door. "There you are at last, Hector," he says. He squints at me. "That's an odd sort of name. What's your other name? Your family name?"

"I haven't got one, I don't think."

"Where's that dog of yours?"

"With Diana," I tell him. I talk about the pipeline we're building from the lake to irrigate the gardens. "Beth thinks we're going to need a pump. Do you have one anywhere around here?" What I have in mind is the small kind of suction pump we use underground to circulate the hot springwater to the bathhouse and the central heating system.

"Maybe you'll need a pump, maybe not," he says. The sun's just gone and his figure is dark against the window. "It'll depend on the lake." I'm not sure what he means. Perhaps his concentration's wandering again. But then he says, "There is a pump, but we've never been able to use it. It draws too much power and overloads the generator. They got most things right when they set us up here. The wrong-sized pump was one of the few slipups."

"How did they know what you'd need? I mean, how long did they think you'd be here like this?"

"Five years. A hundred years? Who knows? As long as it takes, I suppose."

His voice is sounding steady. I decide to ask him more. "You and Beth and Diana keep using that phrase 'when it all happened.' What actually happened?"

But he repeats, his voice querulous again, "Who knows?"

The sky has lost its glow and has become pearly.

It's quite dim in the room. I turn on the table lamp beside his chair and look at the stacks of books on the floor under the table, wondering if he'd like me to read to him.

"I'm not being facetious, Hector," I hear him saying. "Nobody had any idea what had hit us. For months, though, it seemed every day the newspapers had headlines of another disaster. Yet another nuclear accident in the northern hemisphere. A ship sinking and spilling out a load of toxic waste into the sea. Disastrous results from experimental herbicides. It seemed never-ending." I see he is holding his trembling right hand as he speaks. "Then people started dying. Huge numbers of them. Then the newspapers stopped. The television news stopped. No radio news. This silence was the most terrifying thing of all. Near the end, this media silence was broken, but only by the government issuing instructions for the evacuation."

"So nobody ever found out what was causing the deaths?"

"Well, of course everyone had theories in the first few weeks. Toxic buildup in the sea or from insecticides or fertilizers. Perhaps the chemical bush-clearing techniques. Perhaps a drift of nuclear rubbish from the north. It was most likely the gradual accumulation of all these things until the combined effect was just too much for the earth to absorb anymore. But then the panic got so great, there was no time for theories. Evacuation was the main thing. Get the survivors away before everyone was lost."

"Get them away to where? Where have they gone?"

He doesn't reply. "They can't have gone anywhere else in the world. Nowhere was safe."

He looks tired. Perhaps I am tiring him with these questions. He has turned his head and he's looking up at the sky, now a clear blue, slowly darkening. There's a slender white thread of new moon.

"Didn't you try to find out where they were going? What about the people themselves? Didn't they ask where they were being taken?" Evan shakes his head. "I can't believe millions of people would troop off without knowing where they were being taken."

"You have no idea," Evan says, his face still turned away from me, "how bad it was here. People were terrified. I expect they felt that anywhere else would be better. You can't expect people always to behave rationally, even when they're not frightened out of their wits."

He has gained control of his shaking right hand. "I'm tired, Hector," he says. "Can you help me into bed?"

A few weeks ago I wouldn't have been strong enough to do this. He cannot use his legs at all. One of them is horribly scarred and twisted. The other is thin and wasted. The damaged leg is always swollen at the end of the day. I lever the lower half of his body from the chair to the bed as gently as I can, but even so his jaw is clenched and his eyes screwed up with the pain. Beth has told me they think there's a nerve pinched some-where by the badly set bone, but of course there's nothing they can do about it.

"Send Beth in, will you?" he says. His voice is curt.

Perhaps I've annoyed him with questions. I turn as I get to the door and see his face has relaxed and he's smiling at me. "Good night, Hector, and thanks."

DIANA

"Finished!" I shout. We've reached the lake. The last length of pipe lies among the bulrushes not far from the blind, its end in the lake water. Hector won't dance properly when I grab his hands and try to swing him around in a circle. I'd have done better to try to dance with Stewart.

"We've still got to figure out how to get the lake water to run up the pipe," he says. "And some of the connections are a bit weak. They might not hold once the water does start moving."

"Shut up, Hector. We can think about that later. Come and have a swim."

I set off around the lake toward the rocky beach. Hector catches up to me by the time I reach the trail through the swamp. "Evan says there's a pump, but it overloads the generator," he tells me. Stewart's caught up with us. He makes a sudden dive off the trail into the swamp and I grab his collar. "Where's his leash, Hector? He can't go rushing through the swamp."

"I know," Hector says, "the nests." He speaks in a sarcastic voice. I suppose he doesn't believe in them.

"Anyway, the swamp's dangerous. Great-grandfather McGregor disappeared there." He looks interested at that. "He wandered into the swamp and he was never found. It was probably winter, though. The swamp's more swampy then, if you know what I mean."

"Has your father's family always lived here?"

"Generations of them. My grandmother's family was called McGregor, and they built the house early last century, 1910 or so, I think. The lake used to be known as Old McGregor's Lake—if it had any name at all."

"Old McGregor? Evan told me a story about him. Was it true, that story?"

"Of course!" It seems hard to get Hector to believe in anything unless he sees it in a book. "Then Dad's father, who was a Redfern, married into the McGregor family, and the lake was given the official name of Redfern Lake. I suppose that was because both Dad and Granddad Redfern were big-shot ornithologists. Mom says tourists used to come here, just to tiptoe in and peer at the birds. Granddad Redfern made them park their tour buses half an hour's walk away."

We've reached the rocky beach. I'm taking off my sneakers. The T-shirt and shorts I'm wearing will do for swimming. The stones are sparkling in the sunshine, except at the lake edge where they're greenish and darkened by the lapping water.

"Come on," I say to Hector, who's still standing and gazing at the lake, thinking about something.

"Diana," he says, "where do you think all the people went?"

I treat it as a serious question. "We think the most likely place is the moon," I tell him.

He stares at me perfectly still for a second or two. Then he laughs. Loud laughs, and going on and on.

I'm furious and rush out into the water, throwing myself in to drown out the laughter.

HECTOR

The thing with Diana is she's quite normal for ages
and then she suddenly becomes childish and says stupid things. But I shouldn't have laughed at her like
that. I went into the water after her. She went out far
too deep and she can't swim yet. I apologized to her.
I've read about apologies in novels recently. You say
"sorry" to people and they forget about what you've
done wrong, even though you intended to do it all
along. This time it didn't work properly. She was still
angry.

She told me I don't know anything. People had been
visiting the moon for years. Normal people, she told
me, preferred to try to explore the planets and the
stars rather than burrowing into the earth and missing
everything. She told me there'd been a big settlement
on the moon back before everything happened.

It's a shock to me to think of people up there actually walking around on the moon. There's no real
air to breathe up there, I know that much. I've learned
a lot of strange things about life away from the underground—but people on the moon? I can't believe
that. All the same, it might be possible. I decided to
cross-check with Beth later.

Just then Beth appeared at the other side of the lake.
She grabbed the end of the last pipe and held it up out
of the water. "You clowns!" we heard her shouting

across the lake. "The water's pouring down over the gardens and washing half the plants out!"

Another mood change for Diana. "It's working!" she shrieked and grabbed me around my neck. Why does she have to hang onto me whenever she's pleased?

"But I don't understand," I said. "It's impossible for the water to run uphill over the edge of the lake like that."

"Don't be boring," she said, "the lake can do anything."

So we've spent the rest of the day mucking about in the gardens, digging channels to guide the water along the rows, and fitting smaller pipes to guide the water to the other gardens. We get hot and muddy. Diana rushes off to the lake again for another swim when it seems we've got the irrigation organized. Beth says she's starving and she's worried about Evan. She says he's gloomy today, and I worry that my questioning last night might have disturbed him.

We wash the mud off our legs and arms in the lake water flowing gently through the pipe. I walk with Beth up toward the house. I can't resist asking more questions. It's as if something is driving me on. "Why, if everyone was leaving, did Evan think it was safe to stay here?"

"Well, wouldn't you? It's very pleasant here." She smiles at me. She's treating my question lightly. I speak carefully.

"Probably other people liked where they lived too. But they left."

She sees I'm serious. She pauses by the rhododendrons. "Evan always believed it was the bush-clearing process that caused the problem. I don't know when they started this new process, but it would have been well after your people went underground. In the end the whole country was cleared, virtually. It turned into one gigantic market garden to supply the starving world market. By this time, of course, nothing could be grown in Europe that was safe to eat. The demand for food was so great, there never seemed to be enough available land to cultivate. The bush had to be cleared quickly. They chucked chemicals out of helicopters." She shrugs and walks on. "I still get angry about it. There were a few of us who shouted and stood about with banners. But you see, the country was getting very rich. All those overseas currencies flooding in. No tourists anymore, of course, but who needed them? We were all wealthy after a lot of lean years."

We have reached the grassy area near the house. "Evan's family owned all this land, from the lake right up to the foothills of the mountain. Evan was still quite young when all this started, but even so he had a big international name in bird conservation. He'd collected threatened birds from bush reserves—or former reserves anyway—before the bush was destroyed. He brought them here to the lake or to the zoo in the city. He'd managed to save them all."

"They're all still here?"

"Perhaps. I don't know. A lot of them are nocturnal and he always was the only one who could find them, and of course over the last few years he hasn't been able to watch them properly."

"But this bush was saved back then?"

"Evan saved this area somehow. He persuaded the authorities to make the helicopters with their filthy spray remain well to the south of the mountain. Even though 'conservation' had become a dirty word, he had his own way. When it all started to happen, the deaths and the panic, he saw that his birds here were unaffected. The birds in the zoo died with all the other animals. The little gang of cows and chickens that were on this property survived. Livestock everywhere else died. All the animals died—even faster than the people died. So when evacuation became a reality, he decided to stay here."

"He was that sure it was safe here?"

"Yes. He tried to talk other people into staying here with us too, but they wouldn't. Not even his brothers and sister. Everyone else was determined to get away."

"What about the other settlements you talk about? The ones Diana tries to contact every night?" We're getting near the house. I don't want her to stop talking yet.

"Other little groups were set up too in other places that were supposed to be safe. Evan set the precedent, you see. His decision made the authorities realize it was worth leaving a few people here to try and keep something going. For instance, four people stayed in a hospital farther south that purified its own water. And other groups found places they thought would be safe. All the settlements were set up to be self-sufficient. We were given CB radios and we organized a schedule to keep in touch with each other every day. Diana keeps trying, but we haven't heard from any of them for over a year."

We're in the house now. She leans against the door frame and I see there are tears falling from her eyes and running down her cheeks. "It's too horrible to remember," she says, and goes away into Evan's room.

DIANA

This all started last night. Hector and I were looking at some of the magazines stashed away in cartons in his room. We brought them out to the light in the main room. Hector is fascinated with the pictures and Mom starts looking at them too. The magazines are almost twenty-five years old. They've got pages of television and radio programs, and there are book reviews and reviews of plays and films and I see that look coming on Mom's face. On the cover of one of them are two people on horses galloping over a hillside. "That's what we need," I say then, because I'm reminded of my broken-beyond-repair wingset.

That's when Mom remembers the bikes in the wonder shed. She says they're all packed up but it wouldn't be hard to put them together and get them going.

So here we are this morning, Hector and I, wobbling about in circles on the grass outside the house, trying to balance on these skinny wheels. I do not want to fall off more times than Hector.

Suddenly I've got it. These things work. They do stay upright as long as you keep them moving. The only trouble is that Hector seems to have figured his out at the same time as I do. We're both flying around on our bikes, dodging Stewart, each other, the house, the rhododendrons.

"Come on," I shout, and head for the path to the lake. Behind me there's an awful crash and a roar of pain. I stop, steadying myself with a foot on the ground, and look back. Hector has collided with the side of the grain shed. He's in a heap on the ground, moaning.

HECTOR

Beth comes in with a steaming bowl of water. My leg is resting on a towel on the sofa and it has stopped bleeding. There's blood on my face where I grazed it against the wooden shed.

Evan has been watching the bike-learning from the veranda, and he wheels his chair through the French doors. "Let me look after someone else for once," he says to Beth, and takes the bowl from her. "Go and watch over our fool daughter."

"That girl can look after herself," Beth says, but she goes anyway.

Evan gently sponges away the blood on my face, and then bathes my knee and the long scratch running down to my ankle. "They're only grazes," he says. "There won't be one single scar." He's being very kind and gentle.

"I didn't mean to upset you the other night with all those questions," I say. He doesn't answer, just pats my skin dry with an edge of the towel. "It's just that I can't stop myself from trying to find out." It's like a jigsaw puzzle to me. Slowly I am getting the pieces put together, but the whole picture is not complete yet.

"It's all right," he says. "They're things Beth and I haven't talked about for a long time. It's the only way we can cope, you see, getting on with day-to-day life and not yearning after the past. It would have been bad enough, of course, if this hadn't happened." He taps his damaged leg. "But because it did, it's been so very much worse for Beth."

"She told me about you saving the birds and everything. Them dropping stuff on the bush."

"That was just the start of it. Years later when suddenly overnight it seemed all the animal life and half the human life was dying all over the planet, there was just no time to find out why and try to correct the situation. It was happening too fast." He smiles. "Besides, life had been pretty good for a while. The late 1990's and the turn of the century were exciting times to be living, in many ways. We were all rich—there was plenty of money around down here in the southern hemisphere. We were supplying food for the whole world. The threat of nuclear war was gone—"

"Really?"

"Oh, yes. What a victory that was. The world disarmament treaties were signed and carried out before the twenty-first century started."

"So there wasn't a nuclear war after all?"

"Never. I'll remember to my dying day the celebrations when those treaties were signed."

"But," I say, "everyone's dead anyway, more or less."

I've gone too far, I see that immediately. His face becomes crumpled and dark. I've spoken without thinking. The reason we'd all lived underground, after all, was to avoid the wholesale loss of life that nuclear war was bringing, according to the Counselor. Well, the Counselor might not have been right about nuclear war, but it seems to me he was right in the long run.

"You're correct in a way," Evan says at last. "We shouldn't have stopped after our victory over nuclear weapons. There were many more evils that needed defeating. Don't worry, I've had plenty of time to think of that for myself." He's looking out the window, almost talking to himself. "But as for everyone being dead, that's debatable. It really is."

Here I want to ask him about the moon, but Beth's voice sounds from the kitchen, calling to Diana out on the lawn, and Evan's face brightens. "Well," he continues before I can say anything, "we're all here, aren't we? Dear old Beth. You know, Beth was the only one with enough guts to stay here with me. She was marvelous. She was the one who got everything organized."

I like these people, but the trouble is I keep wondering what's happening underground. They were depending on me down there. I wonder if I should go back.

PART
───4───

DIANA

He asks us many questions about our lives, but there's not much information from him about his background. More and more he's been alluding to his underground home as a kind of paradise. Sometimes I feel he's saying we're privileged to have him, he's given up so much by leaving there.

He told me the other day that as kids grow up down there, they are allocated a field of expertise. By expertise he means the various types of knowledge required to keep them alive. He said that he is different from the others however. Because he is the youngest, the last child to be born there, he'd been chosen to train to take the place of their leader in due course. He said all this in a reverential tone, and then he started getting bossy with me about something we were preparing in the kitchen for dinner that night. Big deal. He's sorry that he's given up the chance of being king to a whole lot of underground worms. He needed to throw his weight around at our place.

I think what's really getting him is the idea that

all the people who left here might come back. Perhaps he thinks his underground kingdom will be threatened. I heard him questioning Mom about the moon earlier tonight, and now I wish I'd never mentioned the moon to him.

"Yes, that's our theory," I heard Mom tell him. "It's our hope, really. It's the only hope we've got to cling to. It's a forlorn hope. There certainly was a settlement on the moon that was started in the last century. I know the great powers poured money into space settlements after disarmament, but it's hard to believe they would have had time to prepare the moon settlement for so many people. But don't say anything to Diana. For years now we've said that's where they are. There's no need to tell her yet there might be some doubt about it."

I hate them for not telling me the truth. They've always told me that all the people escaped to the moon. I thought they believed it too.

"Anyway," her voice went on, "while it was no trouble to get up to the moon settlement, I've no certainty they had enough transport to get millions of people up there." She laughed with a scoffing tone. "Perhaps they got a few world leaders up there safely and a couple of army commanders and a weapons inventor. That'd be earthly justice."

I wish I'd never mentioned the moon to him. Now he's upset Mom, and she's said things I've overheard and they've upset me. I wish he'd never come here.

HECTOR

"I know I should go back to the underground." I'm wheeling Evan down to the lake. "I need to go back. I'm sort of missing it."

"Homesick?" Evan asks.

"Is that what it's called? Perhaps. Anyway, they need me there. That's what the Counselor said when they found out Stewart was leading me to the outside."

"What is it really that's making you think of going back? Do you yourself truly want to go or is it because you feel you ought to?"

"I don't know. Anyway, it's probably not a real question. I don't think I can go back. They'd be too suspicious of me. They'd think I've gotten the illness, or that I'd lead people to them who have gotten the illness."

If only things weren't so complicated, I could take Evan underground with me and get his leg treated by the doctor.

"If it's on your mind, Hector, you'll have to sort it out or it'll eat at you."

"I wish I could sneak in there and make sure everything's okay and not be seen."

"Be a fly on the wall, you mean? We've all wished to be that sometime or other."

It's Christmas Day today. Last night we sang Christmas carols. "Silent Night," "Good King Wenceslas," "The Holly and the Ivy." I knew them all. We used to sing them at Christmas in the children's quarters. Perhaps the carols have made me melancholy today. After the carols there was present giving. Beth and Evan gave me some swimming trunks Beth had made and an enormous towel with a picture on it of a man crouching on a plank with a huge curl of water curving up behind him. Beth gave Diana a dress. Diana gave me a silver picture frame. I'm not sure what to do with it. Of course I didn't have presents for anyone but it didn't matter. Evan said the best present I could give him was a walk at dawn to the lake to see the birds.

So here we are. "Sssh," Evan says as we turn the last bend in the trail. "Don't make a noise."

The lake has its silver look in this early light. The bush is still black around it. The birds are everywhere, hundreds of dark shapes against the lake or, higher in the air, reflecting colors in the first light coming over the horizon. I don't know why Evan said to be quiet. The birds would never hear us over the noise they're making.

"Look!" Evan whispers. His body tenses forward. All I can see are a few large duck-like shapes with long plumy tail feathers leaving the bulrushes and scuttling past the blind and on around the lake to the grasses.

"They're still here," Evan says. "Think of it, Hector. They've made it. They're still here."

"Those duck things?"

"*Duck things?* Those duck things, as you call them, have trembled on the edge of extinction for two centuries. Until now."

"Those are some of the birds you saved?"

"They've survived here for seventeen years. That proves a successful transplant. Concludes the final chapter of my book. A happy ending, Hector."

"That's great," I say. I know it's inadequate for his tremendous elation.

We stand still, watching the light creep over the bush. "I've seen enough for now," Evan says. "Let's go back. I know Beth's got something nice for breakfast, seeing that it's Christmas Day."

"That story you told me about the lake," I ask him as I maneuver the wheelchair on the trail, "was it true? Was it about your grandparents?"

"Which story about the lake? I don't remember. The lake's full of stories. I could have told you any one of them."

I can't tell if he's joking or not. On the way back he says, "Thank you, Hector, for a wonderful Christmas present. And I'm sorry you're troubled about whether to return to your community. You're free here, you know, to come and go. You're welcome to live here forever if you like. You're good for me. You're good for us all."

Christmas Day is fun. I forget my melancholy. Just as Beth had coffee hidden away for us to have at breakfast time, Evan has a bottle of red wine. "Very nearly the last," he says as he uncorks it at lunchtime. "I wish I'd been born a wine-maker instead of a bird-watcher," he says. "Think of the cellar we could be laying down if we grew grapes instead of spinach."

Diana mutters to me, "Here comes the wine. Soon

we'll be off down memory lane," as if I might mind that. Diana is wearing the dress Beth made for her. It's blue like the sky with a long skirt using lots of fabric. She looks different. "Perhaps it's very old-fashioned," Beth says. "Who knows these days what everyone's wearing?"

DIANA

Everyone made such a fuss about seeing me in a dress, I nearly took it off right away. But the full skirt swishing around my legs felt good once I got used to it.

Hector must have been talking to Mom and Dad about going back to his underground, because to-night before we all went to bed he made a little speech about how he'd like to accept their offer to stay on here because he'd decided it wouldn't be a good idea to go back to the caves. He said he hoped he'd be able to fit in and help with whatever needed to be done. Then he made a joke and said he'd do anything as long as it didn't involve ever having to go near the bulls. Mom and Dad clapped and cheered and looked very pleased. So it looks as if I've got a new brother.

HECTOR

The day after Christmas, Beth tripped in the big garden and cut her shin on the hoe she was using. We didn't think much of it, least of all Beth. She bathed it up at the house and was back working the garden in minutes.

The sun shines on day after day and there's no hint of rain coming. The irrigation arrangement has been working very well. We leave the top end of the pipe in the lake for a few hours each day and that brings down enough water for all of the gardens. Everything's flourishing. Evan says it's because the plants like the lake water.

The rest of the time we swim in the lake and Diana and I ride the bikes. I haven't fallen off since that first day. Beth has succeeded in teaching us to swim properly. Diana's a natural, as Beth puts it. She can dive better and swim faster than I can. One day I'll find something I can do better than she can.

This morning Diana wakes me early. She says she's going out to milk the cows because Beth's ill. She asks me to get Evan up so he can try to find out what's wrong with Beth. She speaks loudly and with urgency but perhaps it only seems that way because it takes me so long to wake up and listen to her properly. As it is, she's gone before my eyes finally open and for a moment or two I wonder if it was a dream. I get up and go to Evan's room. He's already awake. "Diana said you were coming through to get me," he said.

I slide him into his chair and wheel him along to Beth's room. She's lying in bed, leaning against several pillows, and in the early morning light her face is white and pinched. "It's nothing," she says as we go in, "just a scratch."

"Show me," Evan says.

It's the cut on her shin she got from the hoe. The skin around it is puffy and red. The redness is spreading up to her knee. "It's nothing," she says again. "I'll be up in a few minutes."

"No," I say, "don't move. Stay as still as you can."

Beth gives a little smile. "Yes, sir, anything you say, Doctor Hector," she murmurs.

"Don't mock, Beth, he's right," Evan says. "You jiggle about too much and you'll have the infection running around in your bloodstream. Go and put some water on to boil, Hector."

I go out to the kitchen and fill a pan with hot water. The solar-heated water is halfway to boiling already. I find a clean towel that has worn fine and soft and I'm tearing the hems off when Evan wheels himself into the kitchen. "It's infected," he whispers. "We've got a problem here, Hector."

"I know," I whisper back. "What medical supplies have you got? Any antibiotics? Penicillin?"

He shakes his head. "None. They didn't leave us much in the way of antibiotics. They didn't have much to leave by then. Anyway, it's going on twenty years ago, Hector. These things deteriorate in time." He picks up and tosses down again a tube of antiseptic cream I've put ready on the bench. "That stuff will be useless by now. Nothing left in it but water and rancid glycerine."

"What'll we do?"

"I don't know. I have no idea. Well, for a start, boil that rag you're tearing up. Let it boil for five minutes or so. And boil some more water and put lots of salt in it."

"Salt?"

"Probably the most potent disinfectant we've got."

I do what he says. I notice his left hand trying to control the shaking of his right hand. "I took one risk," he says, "one stupid risk. Trying to get the best out of our last drop of gasoline. One twist on the steering wheel too many. The tractor flipped me out and rolled over me and away on down to bury itself in the gully." I nod. I don't know what to reply. Beth has told me about his accident, but this is the first time he's described it to me himself.

"We could have dug that last little bit of land by hand," he goes on. "A day or two with a shovel."

I sterilize a steel bowl with the cloth in the boiling water. "Beth will be okay," I say.

DIANA

It's nightfall and by now Mom's tossing and feverish. We're boiling things in the kitchen and Dad's changing the dressing from time to time, but even though he's very gentle we can hear her calling out with the pain. She can't eat and she's been sick a few times.

"It's serious," Hector says to me. I don't need him to tell me that.

"There'd be antibiotics in the pharmacy underground that would help," he says.

I don't answer. I don't care about his underground.

"I could go and get something and bring it back,"
he says.

"Really?" Now he's got my attention. But then I
remember. "There wouldn't be any medicine left down
there that would still be any good. It's years and years
older than our stuff, even."

"There are chemists down there," Hector says, "research pharmacists working all the time. They're not
just sitting around down there watching vegetables
grow. They're working, experimenting, making new
things."

"You think they'd give you something to help
Mom?" He's not looking at me, but he nods. "I thought
you'd decided not to go back there again."

"I did. But things have changed, haven't they?"

"When would you go?"

"As soon as it's light. I'll take Stewart. You'll have
to draw me a map."

"Right. I'll do it now. But Hector," I add, "don't
tell Dad where you're going."

HECTOR

I can tell Diana's nearly frantic about her mother. She's
trying to hide it.

At the moment I don't waste time thinking about
how I'll persuade the Counselor to give me the medication. There'll be plenty of time to think out the ex-
act words to use during the long trip. Right now I'm
thinking about getting there. I'll take a bike for the
first part along the old roads and across the fields. I

need Stewart with me as a guide through the maze. I hope he'll remember the way. Perhaps he won't want to remember. Up here he's everybody's favorite. He might remember what the people underground tried to do to him.

There's a problem with using a bike. Stewart won't be able to keep up. So working on the veranda in the lamplight I improvise a kind of carrier for him. He hates the carrier—simply a board attached to the crossbar behind the handlebars. Diana's trying to hold him steady while I get on the bike. I circle on the lawn while he hangs his head over the handlebars and moans heartbreakingly. "Let him run behind you for a while," says hard-hearted Diana. "When he gets tired, he'll be happy enough to sit there."

"Have you drawn me a map yet?"

"Not yet. Hector, if you get morphine or anything like that, you won't give it to Dad, will you?"

"Of course not. But I think you're misjudging him. He's fine now. He's not going to go back on that."

"You weren't here when he was on it. You weren't here when it ran out and he was forced to start getting over it. You don't understand, Hector, he's only now starting to come right. It would be dreadful to undo what he's achieved." She's whispering. The night's still and I know she doesn't want her voice to carry to the room where Evan's watching over Beth.

"Don't worry," I say. "Now what about the map?"

"In a minute," she says.

"Can you cope on your own with what Evan needs, and the milking and everything?" She doesn't answer immediately. "Did you put the flashlight on the re-charger?" I'm wondering if I should take something with me as a kind of gift, like some milk or some of the dark green vegetables we can't grow underground, but then I realize they wouldn't accept things from the outside. They wouldn't think they were safe.

"I'm coming with you, Hector," she says.

I give her the reasons why this is impossible. Beth and Evan can't be left alone for a whole day. It might be dangerous for her to come with me. I don't know how the people underground are going to treat me, let alone a stranger.

She says it's easier to come with me than try to draw a map I probably wouldn't be able to follow. "And once you're there, Hector, you never know, they might be so glad to have you back, they won't let you go. I'll be there to bring the medicine back for Mom."

I refuse to take her with me. She says she's not going to draw the map, so she'll have to go with me or I'll never be able to find the way. I say there's no hope of getting medicine for Beth if I don't go. It's a bit of a deadlock. It seems we need each other.

The sun will rise in a few hours. "Anyway," she says, "if they do give you the medicine, you're not going to be able to rush off with it right away, are you? You'll have to talk to everybody for a while. It's only polite and anyway, you'll want to, won't you? I could come straight back with the stuff for Mom while you sit around and chat."

Sit around and chat? I wonder what sort of picture of underground she has in her mind.

"I'll set the alarm for dawn, and I'll do the milking while you boil some eggs and get some rice and vegetables ready for Dad during the day," Diana continues. "And you can get some food together for us to take. We can be ready to leave by the time the sun's rising. You should get some sleep now. And wear long jeans tomorrow. Remember the blackberry."

She goes inside. I follow her, still trying to argue. I hear her telling Evan what she intends everybody to do tomorrow. If this country still had an army, she'd be running it.

DIANA

As I predicted, Stewart got tired after ten minutes of trundling along behind our bikes. During the night I found a big cane basket, which I tied to the back of Hector's bike, and we put Stewart in that. Of course he's too big to put on a bike. It takes Hector time to get used to balancing the extra weight and Stewart doesn't look very comfortable, but we can't go without him.

We go back along the roads and across the paddocks Hector is seeing for the first time in daylight. The ground is getting steeper and the blackberry is closing in. We leave the bikes and start walking. I hear Hector behind me saying something about putting Stewart's leash on him before we get into the bush, and then his voice stops suddenly. When I look around, he's staring back across the valley. "Diana, what's that?" he asks.

From up here you can see the sea, a sharp line along the paler blue of the sky at the horizon. I tell him, "It's the sea," and he says, "So we're that close to it."

"I've flown much closer to the coast in the wingset. I've gone low enough to see the rocks on the sand and the breakers. And look over there." I point farther east. "The city's just past those hills. You can see that tall factory smokestack if you really try—can you make it out?—it looks like it's in the sea."

Hector seems to be transfixed by the sight of the sea. He doesn't move for minutes.

"Hector, we can't hang around. Come on." I keep on tramping toward the bush. There's a long way to go.

He catches up, trailing Stewart, who is now attached to his leash. "Look, when we get there, you'd better wait for me in the tunnel with Stewart. Don't let them see you."

"Well, okay. But you'll get the stuff for Mom right away, won't you?"

"Yes, yes, I will."

"How long should I wait there? I mean, if you don't come back immediately, how long should I wait before coming after you?"

"Don't come after me, whatever you do." He looks worried.

"I'll have to do something, Hector. I can't wait for hours without knowing what's happened. Hector? How long should I wait?"

"Look, it'll be all right." He doesn't sound very sure. I realize he hasn't got much idea of what's going to happen. I stop walking and grab his arm.

"Hector, we should have a proper plan. This is life or death for Mom."

He shakes my hand off his arm. "I said it'll be all right, Diana."

We walk on. We pass the worst of the gorse and go down a slope to the riverbed. By now it's completely dried up. The gray rounded rocks tip when we step on them and grate against each other. "It's hard walking on these stones," Hector says. They are the first words between us for quite a while.

"I know. But it's the easiest way to get through the bush." The dark bush crowds each side of the riverbed. "Usually there's a lot of water rushing down here. But look, there's no more snow left on the mountain. It's the first time I've seen it without any snow."

"The mountain?" Hector says. "Where's the mountain?" He's never seen the mountain, with snow or without. From our place it's hidden by the ranges. From here though the peak is visible over the treetops. I point it out to him. "Is that all?" he says. "It doesn't look like much."

"Not from here it doesn't. But from farther away or if you're up in the air you can see how huge it is. It towers over everything." The first time I ever saw the mountain, which wasn't so very long ago, was from my wingset. It was early morning, and the snow on it looked pink. I thought it was the most beautiful and most frightening thing in the world.

We plod on again. It can't be much farther now before we branch off through the bush to the clearing.

"I flew quite close to the city once. I didn't stay around there long. I was scared that something might go wrong with the wingset and I'd be forced to land."

"Why? Wouldn't you be able to take off again?"

"It wasn't that, it was the illness. Mom said the cities were the worst places."

"But there's no one there now, surely."

"Of course not, but there'd be, you know, dead bodies lying about. Skeletons. Mom said near the end there wasn't time for burying."

"Skeletons wouldn't hurt you, would they?"

"They might. Who knows how long the illness hangs around? Anyway I didn't fly low enough to see if there were any skeletons. But it was strange and sort of spooky to see all those buildings and houses and streets crisscrossing each other. To think that once they were full of thousands of people."

"Are you going to fix the wingset?"

"I hope so. I haven't been able to find any more plastic fabric to fix the tear. And I need some more polyklite for the broken strut." It's the polyklite that's the real problem, the steel-strength plastic that makes the wingset so light and maneuverable. I've found some sheets of it, but I don't know if a strip cut off a sheet of polyklite will work as well as the specially molded struts.

My brain gets deep into the problem and I nearly miss the place to leave the riverbed. It's Stewart who changes direction first and leads us into the bush. "We're nearly there," I say to Hector.

HECTOR

We're nearly there. I'm nervous. I delay the immediacy of the underground confrontation by thinking about, instead, how very much I want to go and look at the sea and the abandoned city and I want to see the mountain towering over the ranges.

Here is the clearing. There is the tree I first saw Diana in. Stewart finds the entrance to the tunnels all too quickly. He lies down beside it, his jowls resting on his front paws, his eyes going from me to Diana and back again. He's asking if we're sure we want to go farther.

"Do you think Stewart's got his sight back?" I ask Diana. These days when he looks at me his eyes seem to focus on mine instead of his nose pointing somewhere in the direction of my voice.

"Perhaps. I don't know. Hector, we've got to keep going." Diana has an anxiety in her voice I haven't heard before, even when she was hurrying me along during the night she first took me to the lake.

"Shall we eat something before we go in?" I ask. Diana's still carrying the bag with food and drink in it.

"Let's just get going." She takes the flashlight out and leaves the bag propped against the rock in the shadow.

Stewart leads us into the darkness. Almost at once we're descending sharply. I can see nothing until Diana hands me the flashlight and I snap it on. I remember the narrow corner where the ceiling is very low. After

133

that point the tunnel continues downward, always twisting, forking off in two and sometimes three different directions. Stewart doesn't hesitate. The walls become damper as we wind further downward. They glisten in the glow of the flashlight. I shine the light upward to the pointed ceiling of the tunnel—but only once. "Don't look up," I say to Diana. I've seen the shiny bodies of hundreds of insects, moving restlessly above our heads. Underground beetles, I suppose, and centipedes and worms and spiders. There's a damp smell and the constant murmur of water. Then gradually I distinguish another smell. It's heavily familiar. We're getting close to home.

Diana notices too. "What's that smell?" she says.

"Sssh. We're nearly there."

"But I don't remember that smell being so strong," she whispers.

"You haven't been so close before."

"Yes, I have. Look." She takes hold of my wrist and points the flashlight along the wall ahead. There are the piled rocks, the pushed-back wire in its frame.

"Perhaps you'd better wait here with Stewart." I hand her the light and Stewart's leash. "I can find my way from here. Turn the flashlight off." She does. After a few seconds of blackness there's a glow from the tunnel ahead. "Wait here," I say again. "Stewart, stay here, boy."

He's not intending to come with me. He's sitting folded against Diana's leg, one eye peering around her shin at me. I turn and take a couple of steps toward the glow.

Suddenly there's a blast of light. I'm blinded. I hear Diana gasp and when I look up I see two figures, black shapes against the glare. I glance back at Diana. She's crouching, her hands covering her eyes. There's no sign of Stewart.

"It is Hector," one of the shapes says. I know the voice. "Welcome home, Hector."

"Is there anyone else with you, Hector, apart from her?" the other shape says. I know that voice too.

"No," I say, "just us." The brilliant light dims and dies away.

"Come with us, then," the first voice says.

"Wait for me here, Diana."

"Both of you had better come along," I hear. Diana walks up and stands beside me. I feel her hand holding mine. "Come on, then," she says.

DIANA

The smell becomes stronger. One of the two men walks on ahead and the other follows us. When Hector and I walk past, the one who is following presses back against the rocky wall of the tunnel, his face averted. I've seen nothing of these men's faces yet. I've seen that they are wearing long gowns like the tunic Hector wore. Even in this dim light I can see the gleam of the embroidery around the edges of the gowns at the neckline, hem, and the ends of the sleeves. The man who leads us has a silver thread in his embroidered design and it glitters as we walk closer to the source of the glow. His hair is white. He walks like an old man.

A final corner. There's a wall made of wood cut to fit the irregular shape of the tunnel with a small light above a closed door. The man in front pushes the door open and closes it behind him, shutting us out. In a few moments it opens again and he reappears, placing on the ground in front of us two heaps of clear plastic. Hector picks one up. It's a triangular envelope of flexible plastic, which will fit over our heads and cover us to the ground. There's a circle of mesh near the top of the triangle. I suppose that's for us to breathe through.

"I'm not putting that thing on. It's like a shroud," I whisper to Hector.

"Please, Diana. Understand, they're terrified of the illness. They don't know yet they're safe from us."

"I'm not putting it on."

"It won't hurt you. There's nothing wrong with these things. We always wear them when we're working near the generator." I still refuse. "Diana," Hector goes on, "it might be the only way to get the medicine for Beth."

The plastic things are made to zip shut under our feet. Hector and I have to zip each other's envelope shut with our hands made clumsy by the enclosing plastic, and then help each other stand up again. It's possible to walk, but only just. I follow Hector's example and jam my feet into the two bottom corners of the triangle and swing them sideways. We shuffle forward somehow and go through the narrow door. We must look very stupid.

I concentrate on how difficult it is to walk, and try to keep my fear away.

We seem to be in a long narrow room. Here and there I can see a light and a small glow surrounding it. Mostly it's all in shadow. I thought the plastic envelope might keep out the stench, but it filters through the complex mesh arrangement over my face.

There is nobody around. The men with us have vanished. I'm following Hector. We're walking along wooden planks laid side by side on the dirt floor. Sometimes I see shadowy faces watching us through doors leading off each side of the walkway. "Hector, how much farther?" He doesn't answer. Perhaps my voice can't get out. I'm losing track of time. I want to be back home before dark.

Hector stops in front of a door. He taps his plastic-covered knuckle against the door just once and then gently pushes it open. We go inside.

There's music playing very quietly, a piano and a woman singing. There's someone, a man I think, sitting on a fat comfortable chair with lots of cushions. The only light in the room comes from a lamp on the table beside him. It throws a small glow on the open book he is holding on his knees, but I cannot see his face. I can't even see how big the room is, because the walls are dissolved away into shadows. I have plenty of time to look around because neither Hector nor the man says anything for ages.

At last the man speaks. I have to strain to hear. It's that quiet breathy voice that reminds me of the way Hector used to speak. "You may go to your room,

137

Hector. I shall send Felix to you presently. You must stay strictly in your room until Felix says you are well. I am quite certain you would not have been irresponsible enough to return here knowing you were bringing illness with you. But I want time to reassure the rest of the community." The music stops with a few soft clicks. Silence again.

"Very well," Hector says.

"Hector, what about the medicine for Mom?" He seems to be shaking his head at me through the plastic. I turn to the figure in the chair. "Hector said you'd have something here to help my mother. She's very ill—tell him, Hector."

It's as if I don't exist. Neither of them takes any notice of me. Hector goes toward the door, opens it, and beckons me to follow him with a sharp movement of his head. Once outside the door I make him listen to me. "What's going on, Hector? What's all this about sitting in your room? Why didn't you ask him? Hector, *what about Mom's medicine?*"

"Quiet, Diana," he mumbles. "Come on, this way." I notice more doors ajar, more sinister shadows watching us. My voice still seems to be echoing around the walls. I follow him through a long stretch of tunnel, which has no light at all, to another group of doors. We go in one of them. "My room," he says. "Close the door."

In the darkness I think I can make out the shape of a chair. I sit down, feeling peculiar suddenly. It's as if there's not enough air to breathe properly. "I'm taking this thing off, Hector. Help me with the zipper."

138

We help each other out of the plastic garments and leave them lying on the floor. It's still too hot and humid. "Right," I try again. "What's going on?"

"Please keep your voice down, Diana."

"Why? Why does everyone whisper down here?"

"I don't know. We just do. Everyone will have heard you by now, that's for sure."

"Does it matter?"

"We'll talk to Felix about Beth. He's the chief medical officer. It's Lark, one of his assistants, who's been developing new antibiotics."

"When will Felix get here?"

"Soon."

I'm starting to twitch with impatience. "Can't we go and find him?"

"No. We have to wait here."

"It could be hours. That guy didn't look as if he was in a hurry about going to fetch him. Hector, I'll have to leave soon if I'm going to get back to the house before it's dark outside."

"I know."

We wait. I ask Hector about the man in the big armchair.

"That is the Counselor," Hector says. I notice suddenly that his voice is slowly returning to the way it was when I first met him. "He is the one I told you about. You should not have talked to him, Diana."

"Why ever not?"

"We never talk directly to the Counselor."

"Is he deaf or something?"

"Of course not. It's that we must not annoy him."

"Why would talking to him annoy him?"

"We do not do that, that's all. He talks to us. It's the way it is here."

I don't like it here at all. I want to get away as soon as possible. I'd go on my own to find this Felix except that I don't want to be alone in these weird passages.

"I'm worried, Diana. There's something wrong here."

"What do you mean? The way people are hiding and peering out of doorways?"

"What? Oh, no, that's quite normal. I mean the smell."

"You noticed?"

"I thought it was just because I've been away for a while. There has always been a smell like that from the generator. But it seems a hundred times worse now. It seems to be everywhere."

"From the generator? Whatever sort of generator is it to have a smell like that? And anyway, if you've got a generator, why does it have to be so dark? What have you all got against being able to see properly?"

"We can see all right." He speaks in his don't-criticize-my-place tone.

There's a single tap on the door. It swings open and a small man comes in. He looks ancient. "My dear Hector," he says. "How well you look. Not at all as if you need a doctor." His eyes turn to me. He's got a white beard and long silvery hair. His skin is white and glossy. His gown has the silver threads woven into it I had noticed on one of the first two men.

"We are well, Felix," Hector says. "We don't need any tests or anything."

Felix stops staring at me and turns to Hector, his finger to his lips, signaling to him to be quiet. He opens the little case he is carrying and gets out a writing pad and a pen. He's scribbling on a sheet of paper as he talks on in a normal voice. Normal, I mean, for down here.

"Well, certainly my initial examination shows nothing wrong with you. I think we can safely dispense with those plastic mummy cases now. But you both need a warm drink with a drop of my famous tonic, I think. Will you come with me, please?"

He hands Hector the sheet of paper. He reads it quickly and passes it to me, saying "Of course, Felix." The note says *We can't say anything here. Follow me to the main hall, we can talk there.* Felix takes the paper back from me and tears it into several pieces. He closes his case, and we follow him out of the room.

Hector lets him get a little ahead, then he murmurs close to my ear, "Be careful what you say. He might be spying on us for the Counselor."

I can only stare at him. I'm completely confused.

HECTOR

Life used to be simple here. I knew exactly what to do every day and so did everyone else. Nothing went wrong. Work, food, rest, study, in a perfectly regular cycle. That is how I remember the underground. But now I'm unsure and out of step. Never before in my life have I suspected Felix might be against me.

We're sitting at one of the long tables in the center

of the long hall, empty and still at this time of the day. I'm watching Felix's face as he leans forward and whispers, "Tell me about it, Hector, everything. What's happening out there? What's it like now?"—and I realize that of course Felix is one of the originals, one of the group that was with the community from its beginning. He was born out there. He remembers the outside.

Diana is boiling with impatience. Before she starts in her resounding voice I tell Felix about Beth's leg and her need for some kind of antibiotic, and that I know that's what Lark's been working on. "We have to get medication to her *soon*," I say.

Felix's face is amazed. "But my dear boy, they will never let you leave again."

Diana grows tense beside me. Again to stop her speaking out, I get in first. "Diana will have to take it on her own."

Felix glances around to make sure we're still alone. "Hector, how can you be so sure the Counselor will let Diana go, now that she is here?"

I am silenced by this possibility. Diana's leaning forward and whispering urgently, her eyes never leaving the old man's. "Felix, there are a lot of people down here. At my place there are only Mom and Dad and me. Dad's a cripple stuck in a wheelchair. He's there now on his own trying to look after Mom and he can't even look after himself. They're waiting for me. If I don't go back, they'll both die. And I couldn't bear being without them. You'll have to let me go." She's still holding Felix's gaze. "They couldn't keep me here as a prisoner! I refuse to stay!" Her voice rises.

"In the past, long ago, others refused to stay too. The Counselor usually won." Felix shrugs. "It's not a prison, really. Or if it is, there are worse prisons."

"Hector, do something! This is getting like a nightmare!"

"Shut up, Diana, you'll only make it worse," I say, glancing around.

"Worse? Worse? How can it possibly be any worse?" She buries her face in her arms on the table.

"Felix, you've got to help us. Help her. Look, I brought her down here in good faith, thinking we could help her mother."

"Well, yes, in a normal world we would help."

"Can't you sort it out with the Counselor?"

Felix laughs a little. "Sort it out with the Counselor, oh yes, indeed. Consider for a moment his point of view. So many of the residents of his community are old now. You're the last child to be born down here and you're not exactly a child these days. There are a dozen or so in their twenties, some in their thirties and forties and so on—but most of us old originals, we've long passed our seventies. The Counselor himself is nearly ninety. He's faced with his own imminent mortality. He does not want to contemplate the prospect of the death of his beloved community as well."

"I don't see why that has to involve Diana!"

"Don't you? It's quite simple really, if you think about it. And there's another thing. Diana's been here once. Who's to say she won't come back and bring others with her, possibly to destroy or loot the community? The Counselor is very concerned about security, as we all know."

"She can't bring others back. You heard her say there are only three of them. I know. I've been living there."

"*I* believe you. I'm trying to prepare you for the sort of thing the Counselor will say to Diana."

"Okay, then what are we going to do? I'm still sitting here, you know. Remember me?" Diana breaks in.

"I'll talk to the Counselor. I'll try to convince him. And I'll get Lark to sort out a course of antibiotics for your mother, Diana, in the hope I win the argument. There's a four-day course of tablets, which would be the best, although an initial injection would get the whole process working sooner. But I don't suppose you know how to give injections."

Diana hesitates. "Dad knows how," she says.

"Splendid. Hector, you take Diana back to your room and I shall swing into action."

It's hard to imagine the frail little doctor doing anything so strenuous. I stop him before he leaves to ask him about the smell. As I thought, it's the waste products from the generating system. "The fumes are building up, becoming quite a problem," he tells me. "But the engineers are working on it. They have a plan." He taps the side of his nose, smiles at Diana, and leaves us.

"Let's stay here for a bit longer," I say to Diana. "We can't talk in my room."

"Why can't we?"

"It's the high ceilings of the tunnels. They twist and turn and join up here and there. Little crevices run from room to room and up and down levels. Voices can carry to the most unexpected places."

"So that's why the doctor gave us the note. I thought it was like a spy novel, as if the room was bugged or something."

"He's never done that before."

"I'm going to get away, Hector, whether they give me the stuff for Mom or not. I'm not staying here." I nod. I know she means it. "The flashlight is still there, waiting with Stewart. I can get as far as Stewart on my own."

"I'm going with you," I whisper. I think she doesn't hear me at first, but then she smiles and nods. "I know," she says. "But Hector, what about your mother and father? They must be pleased you're back. Why haven't you seen them yet?"

"Oh, Diana, I'll tell you all about that later. Some other time. It's all different here." I've seen the war of love she has in her family. She couldn't understand the peace of detachment there is in mine.

She frowns, her eyes still asking questions, but she doesn't say any more. We sit here waiting.

DIANA

As I leave the last glimmer of the underground, I turn back and wave at Hector. "Bye!" I shout, enjoying the way my voice rolls around the walls. I don't feel as exuberant as I sound, but I want to lift Hector's despair. I can see his silhouette put hands up to ears in make-believe horror at the noise. "See you tomorrow!" I call, and then I'm in blackness, groping along the damp walls. I come to the chicken wire and feel around the ground for the flashlight, calling "Stewart!" I find the light, but there's no Stewart. I continue along the tunnel, hoping he's around somewhere and that he'll hear my voice soon. One step at a time, I tell myself. The first thing is to get through the maze and on the way home. There'll be time later to think about the other problems.

Still no Stewart. I suppose I shouldn't have expected him to be hanging around waiting. He could be outside after rabbits. I come to the first fork in the tunnel. The maze is starting. Soon the tunnel will be twisting upward in a jagged spiral and branching off in other directions at every turn. I wonder why Hector and I weren't intelligent enough to make some sort of marks to show the way we came through the maze. Bread crumbs, that's what the children used in the fairy tale to leave a trail. I think of Stewart going back later and snuffling up the crumbs, ruining our plans. "Where are you, Stewie?" I shout. I wonder if the old dragon is sitting in his fat armchair hearing my voice echo back through the tunnels. But I prefer not to think about the Counselor now. I have to find Stewart and get out of here. One step at a time.

I know I should be continuing upward. The tunnel divides in front of me. One fork remains level, the other climbs steeply. I take the climbing one. I pick up a sliver of rock and scratch a *D* for Diana on the rock wall of the tunnel. I walk a few more steps and scratch another *D*, every now and then calling for Stewart.

At my third *D* I hear the barking. It's unmistakably the sound of Stewart. It's coming from ahead of me so I must be going the right way—but then the tunnel twists. The flashlight beam throws black shadows that shift eerily as I move. I'm no longer sure about the direction of the sound. It seems to be everywhere. I continue hesitantly now. I think the barking's becoming fainter.

Around another corner. I nearly stumble on something. . . .

My flashlight illuminates two skeletons and I scream loudly. Rags of clothes still adhere to them. There are shreds of hair by the two skulls so close together. They've died with their arms around each other. I stand there for a moment with my eyes closed to calm down my heart, which is thumping in my chest. The twin gleaming skulls are printed on the inside of my eyelids.

I'm going to have to step over them. I don't know if I can. I flash the light beyond them and see that I don't have to. The tunnel ends here. They're lying in a little alcove.

There's a square shape under my foot: an envelope, brown with stains of damp and age. I pick it up and read the blurred writing: *"To whoever finds us."* I put it with the precious package in the pocket of my shirt, turn, and go back the way I've come. I'm still trembling. Today has gone on far, far too long.

I follow the D's back to where I started marking them. I've gone a long way in the wrong direction and I'm beginning to comprehend how utterly lost I am. I stand at the intersection of three passages, each one curving beyond the reach of my flashlight. I'm completely disoriented. There's nothing to show me which way to go. I'm paralyzed because the wrong decision could send me back to the underground. I don't want to go back there until I absolutely have to.

"Stewart!" It's meant to be a shout but my voice breaks on the second syllable and it becomes a wail. The echoes squeal through the passages. Then from somewhere in the distance there's a familiar *woo-ooo-oo* and I know it's Stewart.

I see him by the glow of my flashlight rushing to meet me. I'm so pleased, I forget my fear of the maze. He turns and leads me the right way, upward and through the endless tunnels, past the wrong turnings, and finally outside.

The late sun hurts my eyes and I have to blink and squint and I remember how Hector's eyes used to be. Now that I've been down there I can understand. They save power by making people live in darkness. I think it's not only the darkness that is making my eyes sting now that I'm out in the light. I think it's also the fumes in the air down there.

"Do you want to come with me, Stewart, or wait here?" He lies down outside the tunnel entrance, his nose close to the bag of food I left there earlier. I share the rice cakes with him. My stomach's clenching with hunger, but I give him most of them because I suspect he'll wait here, hoping Hector will appear. What I thought was a bottle of lemon drink turns out to be the unpleasant mixture of milk and water that Stewart loves, and there's a plastic bowl too. I think this morning Hector was packing lunch for Stewart rather than for us. I have a mouthful of the sour liquid and pour the rest into the bowl for Stewart.

An hour's walk and an hour's bike ride. This trail through the bush and along the riverbed is becoming familiar. I'm glad Stewart didn't come with me, because I know that balancing him on the bike isn't easy, and he hates it too. But his company would have been welcome. I can't stop my mind from going over everything. I expect these will be the words I'll write in my diary later.

Someone Hector called Jessyn, a man about Dad's age, came to get Hector after we'd been waiting for an hour. A little later Jessyn came back to get me. We didn't go straight to the Counselor's room; first he took me to the big cave they use as a dining hall, where we'd been earlier with Felix the doctor.

The hall was still in near-darkness, and almost as silent as before, except now I could hear the soft clink of forks and knives against china. As Jessyn and I stood at the entrance to the hall, even those sounds stopped. In the gloom I could see rows of faces slowly turning to stare at us.

I felt a rush of panic and wanted to turn and get

away. I've never seen so many people before. Hector had told me there were a hundred people living here, but a hundred is such a simple complete number—my brain hadn't grasped that a hundred people in reality amounted to this frightening mass of bodies, all with eyes fixed on me.

I wanted to run, as I said, but I was held still by those eyes. I don't know how long the silent staring lasted. Probably only a few seconds. I remember Jessyn gesturing to a plate of food on the end of the table nearest to us, as if inviting me to eat. I shook my head, and he led me out of the hall. I glanced back over my shoulder at the long tables as we left. Every eye was still on us. Nothing else moved. The silence continued.

I followed the glimmer of Jessyn's tunic through the dark passages. Sometimes we had to stoop when the ceiling of the tunnel lowered, and at these points the smell of rotten eggs seemed to have gathered in even stronger, choking clouds. I don't think I'd ever get used to that smell, no matter how long I stayed there.

We walked along the long passageway I remembered from earlier. Each door stood slightly open as before, but now there were no shadowy figures peering out. We reached the Counselor's door and went inside.

Still the pale lamplight fell on the armchair and the knees and hands of the Counselor. This time there was another light shining down on a table that supported a large map. At the edge of its glow I could see Hector, standing by the table, looking at the map.

"I shall not waste time, Diana," said the voice coming from the shadowy figure in the armchair. "I've decided to allow the pharmacy to supply you with the medication your mother requires."

I started to thank him but he silenced me by talking on as if I were invisible. "When I say 'supply,' I don't mean 'give.' This enterprise of mine, this whole underground community, represents an enormous financial investment. My whole inheritance. It was a substantial sum back in the 1960's. I think I'm entitled to a little return on that investment. It's not unreasonable for me to ask for some sort of payment for one of the products of the research division of my community."

"Of course," I broke in, "but please hurry. I must get back—"

He continued speaking as before. "We need a pump."

"A pump?"

"As simple as that. You may take the medicine in return for a pump. A good-quality functional pump."

"Is that all? That's simple. We've got a pump unit we never use."

"It doesn't work, Diana, remember?" Hector spoke for the first time. "It's broken, that's why it's never used."

"That's not true, Hector, we don't use it because it overloads our power supply. I'm sure it would work here." I turned back to the figure. "No problem at all. You're welcome to the pump. We'll drop it back here first thing tomorrow. Now, please, can we get going?"

"No, Diana, you don't understand—" Hector was

being very peculiar, I thought, shaking his head and showing his clenched teeth. Now, of course, I know what he was trying to tell me then.

He turned to the Counselor. "Sir, I need to speak to Diana. May we be excused for a short time?"

"No, Hector, you may not be excused. Please be silent." The aged whisper became cold and commanding. Hector obeyed. "Hector seems determined to alarm you. There is no cause for alarm at all. I shall reassure you. You might care to glance at that map."

To me the map lying on the table was no more than a mass of colored marks. "You see," the Counselor started to say, leaning forward, and I saw him for the first time. He was gray and ill and impossibly ancient. The grayness of his skin darkened to charcoal patches around his eyes, and it was his eyes that were frightening. "Look at the map," he demanded, and I did immediately.

"The red areas are the underground tunnels in which we live," he said. "The blue and yellow lines show the system of underground waterways, hot and cold, and they're shaded with black lines where we've utilized them for our various purposes. Of course the map appears complex because we're dealing with an intricate arrangement of natural systems operating at many levels. The map is not yet complete. As Hector well knows, we don't have a detailed knowledge of the maze that leads to the north entrance. It may be Hector's first major contribution to our community, to map that area for us, before we block off that entrance forever."

He had leaned back into the shadows. I didn't have

to see his eyes anymore. I said as urgently as I could, "This is interesting, but please can I go now?" Again he continued as if I hadn't spoken.

"The blue areas are the features above the ground that are relevant to our community. You'll see the river running north eventually out to sea. To the east you'll see the lake."

It was our lake on that map, a wobbly blue circle near the left-hand side, with both red and black lines leading to it. I looked at the map with more interest, realizing suddenly that this tunnel system actually extends under the Redfern land all the way back to our lake.

"In my university days I was a keen tunnel explorer. I found this whole unknown underground system. Rather like discovering a new land. I knew there had to be some sort of cave system here because of the thermal activity; the steam you could see escaping from among the rocks on cold winter mornings. But I had no idea it would be so vast and so admirably suited for my purposes. I kept the knowledge to myself. My secret land."

I was nearly frantic with impatience. I barely listened to the quavering voice rambling among memories. "When I came into my inheritance, I bought the areas of bush around the main entrances of the tunnel system. So it would remain my secret, you see."

Hector was standing silently by the map, watching the floor. "Where's all this leading to, Hector?" I whispered to him. "How much longer do we have to hang around listening?"

"You'll find out," he muttered.

"Some of the land was hard to buy," the Counselor's voice continued, "because it was government property, a protected area. But enough money in enough hands generally works. I went to a lot of trouble to try to buy the lake area too. There was some nature freak named McGregor who wouldn't let go of the land. It wasn't as if he was using it. He wanted merely to stand around . . . *looking* at it."

He had my full attention now, because of course I knew who McGregor was.

The reminiscent tone stopped. "We've got a problem with disposal of waste material. Over the last year some unexpected chemical reaction has set in and it's getting impossible to live with. The waste chemicals are starting to corrode the metal drums we're using for storage and we think the fumes are toxic. We intend to pump them out into the underground source of the lake."

The lake.

"We need a strong pumping system to force out this toxic material without creating any back flow."

The lake. "You see?" murmured Hector. "About a hundred drums of poison pumped into the lake? Good, eh?"

So there it was. Medicine for Mom, death for the lake.

"Give me the medicine," I said. "You'll get the pump tomorrow."

There were other twists to his bargain. Of the four-day course of antibiotics required for Mom, he's given me enough for only *one* day. The rest I will get on safe delivery of the pump in working order. Hector isn't to come with me. He's to stay there underground while I go home on my own.

Lark, the pharmacist, gave me the small package. She's about forty, pale like everyone else here, with eyes that won't meet mine. "The instructions are inside the package," she said.

So here I am, trudging over the stones in the riverbed toward where the bikes are waiting. The sun hasn't vanished yet over the ranges. I'll be home before it's dark.

HECTOR

I tried to explain to the Counselor what the destruction of the lake meant. The last little oasis in the whole country, perhaps the whole world. Destroy the lake and it'll be the destruction of Evan too. He's stuck in a wheelchair, but he's alive with the success of his whole life's dream.

The Counselor hardly listened. He's got a whole life's dream too. He's not going to waste time on someone else's.

Diana went off triumphantly shouting back at me with one day's medication buttoned in her shirt pocket. I have to wait down here for the ruin of her world.

155

"Diana? Are you asleep?"

"No, no, I'm fine!" I think I was asleep. Dad's beside me in his chair.

"Go and have some rest," he says. "I'll wake you before it's light. Go on."

"I can't." I start reciting the list of things that must be done.

He interrupts. "Go and sleep," he says. "I'll watch over Beth tonight."

I argue that he'll have to watch her all day tomorrow while I go to the caves, but I'm too tired to keep on talking. I go and sleep, as he tells me.

Only seconds later, it seems, Dad is waking me. "It's nearly sunrise, Diana." It's well after daybreak. The sky's light. "Don't panic," he says. "I've fed the chickens. All you have to do is milk the cows. I can't quite manage that yet."

He has managed to do all the other things on my mental list. Even the large wooden clock is ticking again and showing the same time as the other two. When I go outside, I see he's brought the pump up to the house and left it beside the bike. He hadn't been able to tell me, but he'd gotten it ready to go.

I come back to the kitchen with the can of milk from the cows. Dad's reaching up from his wheelchair cooking eggs and steaming rice. He says only that I must have a good breakfast. I sit down on the stool by the bench. I'm still sleepy. "Dad, I'm sorry about the lake. They gave me a hard choice."

"It was no choice at all. You did the only possible

158

thing. Of course saving Beth is the only thing to think about."

"What'll happen to the lake? What about the birds?"

He doesn't answer. On the bench in front of me he puts a bowl of rice with an egg and sliced tomato. "Eat," he says.

I realize he's quite better now, almost like the old Dad. Exactly like the old Dad if it weren't for the wheelchair. I smile at him but he's fussing with something at the sink and doesn't notice.

"How was Mom during the night?"

"Sleeping, mostly, for once," he says. "The fever's gone down a little, but her leg's still looking very bad. They didn't send any ointment to dress the cut?"

"They didn't mention anything like that."

"And only one pill a day?"

"That's right, they said there were instructions. I forgot. I was so sleepy last night." I look around for the package I'd broken open and discarded. It had slithered off the bench and dropped onto the floor. I bend down to pick it up and see another capsule has fallen out of the torn corner. "Here's another one!" I try to open the package further.

"Use some scissors, for heaven's sake." Dad gets some out of a drawer and hands them to me. Two more capsules spill out, and a tiny clear plastic vial. I open out the tightly folded brown papers that have formed the parcel. There's a handwritten note at the center.

"These must be the instructions," I say, and I hand the note to Dad.

He reads for a few seconds, then glances at me. "Not only instructions. Shall I read the note to you?"

I nod.

"My dear brave Diana," he starts, glancing at me again, one eyebrow lifting. "The Counselor instructed me to supply you with one day's course of this medication. (He told me the remainder of the course would not be required.) Instead I have supplied you with the full four-day course plus the serum to be injected during the first twenty-four hours of the course. I can only pray you have a syringe. If I pack one for you it would make the package too large and might arouse the Counselor's suspicions.

"Don't come back with the pump, Diana. Don't come back at all. He has no intention of letting you leave again. That's why he told me that the balance of the medication would not be required.

"My very best wishes to you and yours. Felix."

I don't have to go back there. I feel as if a burden has been lifted off me and the long, beautiful day stretches ahead of me. I get up and put my arms around Dad's neck. His hand thumps my back gently.

"Get me a syringe," he says. "There are some unopened ones in the sewing room somewhere."

I find a syringe, and we go together into Mom's room to give her the injection. She's awake, and smiles weakly when she sees me. "You'll be well again soon," I tell her.

Dad's hands are unsteady as he tears the plastic off

160

the syringe. He stops for a moment, taking two deep breaths, and when he breaks the top off the vial and draws the liquid into the syringe, his hands are firm again. He holds the syringe up to the light and squirts a drop of the liquid out.

I hold Mom's hand as he gives her the injection in her arm. "Was it hard for you to go down underground and get these things for me?" she asks.

"No, Mom, it was okay. Not hard at all."

"Where's Hector?"

"Hector decided to stay with his own people," Dad says to her.

"Oh. Oh well, if that's where he's happiest . . . what about Stewart?"

"Stewart's there too," Dad says.

"We could have looked after Stewart for him . . ."

"Try and rest," Dad says to her. "You just have to relax and let all this medicine take its course."

"But Stewart was happy here. Fresh air and sunshine, dogs are happiest in the open air . . ." her voice stops and she drifts off to sleep. I let her hand go. Dad wheels over to the windows and pulls the curtains across to shade her from the strong morning sunlight.

"I'll check the gardens," I say to Dad. "Give them some water." We smile at each other. "And I'll put the pump back in the shed." We know the lake is no longer threatened.

HECTOR

It's thirty hours since she left. She should have been back a long time ago. I've suggested taking the medications and going to meet her. I said she's probably having trouble with the heavy pump, even though I know it's made of the new polyklite plastic that no one down here has even heard of and is not heavy at all. It will be a lot easier to balance on a bike than Stewart was. Anyway it doesn't make any difference what suggestions I make. They won't let me go. I'm being watched all the time. There was someone on guard outside the door of my room overnight.

My jeans and shirt disappeared during the night, replaced by a tunic. Nobody has said anything about the jeans. I suppose I'll never get them back. My hands feel lost without pockets as I wander around waiting.

I'm summoned to the Counselor's room. "Your little friend seems to have been delayed," he says. "I am surprised. I thought she was keen to get her mother well again. That is quite understandable, of course. Every hand to the wheel is important in such a primitive way of life."

"Perhaps Beth got better without the medication," I say.

"Perhaps she died," he answers immediately.

I haven't wanted to think about this reason. The callous way he suggests it takes my breath away for a moment.

"You don't even care if she dies," I say finally.

"Care? Of course I do not care. You start caring about people and where does it lead? I shall tell you, Hector. It leads to hurt feelings, to arguments, to wars."

He is going to start a long session of counseling. I can recognize his method now. Change the subject by wandering off into philosophical discourse. This time I want to stay with the subject. "You won't get the pump if she doesn't come back."

"We do not need the pump."

"Don't need the pump—what do you mean? Why did you send Diana to get it, if you don't even need it?"

He doesn't seem to hear me. He gestures toward the table where sheets of plans and drawings of the excavations cover the map. "We are using our original plan of interlocking chambers and a pipeline to the source of the lake. We go ahead with disposing of the waste tomorrow."

I have one last try to change his mind. "Isn't there any other outlet you could use? Couldn't we just bury the stuff?"

"Indeed not. The pipeline is nearly ready. Besides," he pauses, and I think he might have laughed, "it will give me a certain pleasure to pump toxic waste into that lake. A kind of divine revenge against old McGregor," and he really does laugh, a kind of wheezing, which turns into racking coughs. I suppose I hate him. That's why I hope the coughing goes on until he expires. The coughs subside into tortured gasps for air. "I shall fetch Felix," I say unwillingly. I turn toward the door.

"Stay!" he wheezes. "Stay until you are told to leave!"

I wait. He doesn't say anything. I can't see him but I can hear his breathing and after a while I wonder if he has dropped off to sleep. I start to move cautiously toward the door again but his voice stops me. He speaks slowly, weightily.

"I am starting to have severe doubts about your suitability to succeed me," he says. "You are showing distressing signs of unreliability, a lack of willingness to assume your part in our design."

"There's no need for it all to go on anymore, don't you see? There's no sickness out there now, at least not in this area. We could leave here. We could take what we want from here and leave the caves forever!"

"In my presence speak only when you're invited to." He leans forward into the light and I get the full blast of his eyes. "We need nothing the outside world has to offer. *Nothing.*" He leans back and his voice becomes milder. "Of course we don't need that pump. We could make a hundred pumps if we needed them. I sent the girl to get the pump because of the pleasure it gave me to imagine old McGregor's face when she told him what it's wanted for. That's why I sent her back. I wanted to make sure old McGregor knows that I won in the end. He wouldn't sell me the lake, but I have claimed it finally."

I can't believe what I'm hearing. "But don't you realize that old McGregor is dead? He's *long* since dead."

164

"Dead?" For once his voice is questioning and uncertain. "He cannot be dead." The Counselor has forgotten that time passes in the real world just as it does here. I wonder if his mind is unhinged.

"He is dead. It's his grandson and his family who live there now."

The Counselor regains his assurance. "It's a pity the girl did not return. She would have had certain uses to us. But we don't need her either."

"She wouldn't have stayed here!"

"She would not have had any choice."

It takes me a moment to understand this.

"You mean you had no intention of giving her the rest of the medication."

"Of course not," the Counselor says. "It was Felix's idea. Give her only one day's supply for her mother, he said, and she will certainly return for the rest. It seemed like a good idea at the time."

Felix's idea. I'd been right to distrust Felix. He's clearly no ally of mine.

The Counselor says some more things to me, sliding into the benign voice he usually uses. I stop listening and realize I must hope Diana won't come back here. I send my thoughts up through the maze and down the valley to her. *Stay away . . . stay away . . . stay away. . . .*

The Counselor drones on. I can hardly bear to stand still anymore in the same room with him. Finally he dismisses me and I escape out into the main tunnel, but the air's no better out here.

DIANA

It's over thirty hours since I left the tunnels. I hope Hector is all right. He was here only a couple of months, but now that he's gone, I miss him.

I'm sorting out the laundry. It's only a gesture, I don't intend to wash any of it. There's no need to, anyway. We've got enough sheets and towels and clothes and things to last six months. I said to Mom once we could leave all the washing to pile up and do it only twice a year. She said this solitary life was turning me into an anarchist. Matilda's pouncing on things as I toss them into different heaps on the floor. She has gradually become part of the household and nobody minds, not even Dad. Here's the blue dress I wore on Christmas Day, just five days ago. Seems like twenty-five.

I'm worried about Stewart. Maybe he's still waiting for me. He'll be getting hungry. Perhaps I should go and get him, but then he might not come back with me. He might have gone to join Hector. I remember though that they tried to get rid of him once before. Stewart's a worry. If my wingset were working, I could swoop down to the clearing and see what's happening. Tomorrow I'll get Dad to look at it—perhaps it can be fixed.

There's a crackle in the pocket of the shirt I wore yesterday. It's the envelope I found in the tunnels. When I close my eyes, I can see the two white skulls

166

close together. I'd pushed the memory out of my mind until now.

I open the envelope. The flap's not stuck down, or if it was, the glue has melted away. There are two pages of close writing inside. It's hard to read. The ink is faded and blurred by damp.

When you find this, get the police, get the army, get whatever it takes to rescue the people imprisoned down here in the tunnels. You know who we are. We're the people who've been disappearing over the last year. You must have noticed. Someone must have realized by now it wasn't all coincidence that doctors, scientists, physicists, engineers, artists, musicians, and so on were dropping out of sight. Some of us must have been missed.

Even if you have noticed, it wouldn't be easy for you to follow the trail. He swore us to secrecy, flattered us by saying we were a chosen few selected by "the authorities" to continue human endeavor beyond what he asserted was certain global destruction within eight months. We all fell for it. He had a strength of argument and a commanding presence, and his story was backed with what appeared to be authentic documents and an endless supply of finance.

We were lured by superb research facilities and the best materials and equipment in the world. Those things are certainly here. But now we don't believe the rest of it.

We found out we are not able to leave if we wish. Some of us brought children and spouses with us. The families have all been split up. The petty tyrannies he imposed—like strict hours for sleeping, eating, and working—I suppose we could tolerate, thinking as we did at first that this was all temporary anyway. But the lack of freedom to leave if we wish and the isolation from loved ones became too much. He said his name wasn't John Smith and told us to call him "Counselor." We realized that in his mind this isn't a temporary community to last five years at the most. This is his empire, and it is to exist forever.

He's crazy to think this place can last forever. The biochemical generator has a safe life of ten, maybe twenty years. After that the chemical buildup will become dangerous. The hydroponic gardens can't last long without massive chemical boosts, and there also the result will be a dangerous chemical effluent.

In fifty years or so this whole cave complex will be seething with toxic gases and poisonous fluid wastes.

We've tried to tell him, but he won't listen.

He has a schedule for human procreation and to this end the women between twelve and forty-five live separately. He intends to choose parental couples according to some mad scheme of his own and the resultant children will be brought up never knowing who their parents are. His dream is to put into practice the perfect education system, he told us proudly the night this grand scheme was un-

folded to us; he intends to educate the children himself. There was an obvious madness in his face when he said this. So, please, if only for the sake of the children, rescue us.

How can he keep us here, all terrified? It's hard to explain. He weaves deception among us so none of us knows who can be trusted. We know he has put spies among us but we don't know who they are. Most of us here are scientists, and fairly young. There's not been time for us to think about power and manipulating people. The most manipulative thing we've ever attempted is to wheedle a bit of research money out of a university department. We call him Führer behind his back, then cower like schoolchildren when his eyes touch us.

Don't disbelieve this letter just because it seems fantastic and incoherent. There isn't time to explain it more fully. The two of us are lost in this dreadful maze of tunnels, writing by the light from the last inch of our last candle. We're hungry and cold, and we don't think we'll ever find our way out.

He's keeping us down in these caves against our will. Many of us want to leave. We don't care how foolish we look for believing him and thinking we had some right to survive while everyone else dies. We want to take our chances with everyone else. Nothing could be worse than being imprisoned in a dungeon with a madman.

Amy Kruger
John Purdue
January 1969

169

Fifty-six years ago those people died trying to find help. I take the letter through to Mom's room where Dad sits watching her sleep. I give it to him and perch on the windowsill while he reads. "Amy Kruger, John Purdue," he murmurs at last. "I know both those names. It's a small world, Diana, as we used to say."

"Small world?"

"It's what you'd say if you were traveling, for instance, among millions of strangers on the other side of the world, and got on a plane from Los Angeles to New York and found yourself sitting next to the librarian from your hometown." He smiles at Mom, who has now woken up. "Which is how I had the first conversation with Beth."

"His first words," Mom says, "were 'what a small world.' So profound. So romantic."

"Well," Dad says, "I couldn't think of what else to say. I was shy."

"Shy," Mom says, scoffing. "Anyway, who were those two people you knew?"

"I didn't know them myself, I said I knew the names. John Purdue's in particular. Amy Kruger wrote a book on alternative energy systems that was very important for years. But John Purdue was my father's best friend when they were students. Dad told me about him because he used to bring him here years ago to look at the grasses and weeds growing in the lake. His field was hydroponics, growing things in water."

"But you didn't meet him?" I ask.

"My father told me he died, quite young, long before I was born. It was said he disappeared while

170

studying something in Brazil. I probably wouldn't have recalled his name except this letter mentions hydroponics.''

"Disappeared in Brazil?''

"That's what everybody thought.''

"Look, I know I came in late on this conversation, but what are you two *talking* about?'' Mom breaks in.

"Sorry, darling,'' Dad says. "Here, read this. No, better that you read it out, Diana.''

I read the letter aloud. "I remember the things Hector said about the underground community,'' Mom says when I've finished. "This letter seems to fit with what he said. But it's so much more sinister. Where did the letter come from?''

"Diana found it,'' Dad says. "With what were apparently the remains of the authors.''

Mom looks at me for a minute and says I've been living an adventurous life while she's been lying around in bed.

"I don't know what we can do about this now,'' Dad says. "It's a bit bizarre to get a distress signal that's over fifty years old.''

"Well, if Hector wanted to stay there, perhaps they're all quite happy now. He always said good things about it, Diana.''

"Yes,'' I say dubiously.

Mom picks up the tone of doubt in my voice. "All the same . . .'' She doesn't finish the sentence, and she sounds uneasy. And she doesn't know half of what happened while I was underground. Dad knows it all, but I haven't told Mom yet.

171

Dad has been quiet, staring out of the window into the dusk.

"Can you stay with Beth, Diana? I'm going out for a while. I'm going to visit the lake."

"In the morning, Dad, can you look at my wingset? It got damaged and—"

"It's okay," he says, "I've seen it. I've fitted two new struts. I found a strip of the fabric for the torn wing too. You can just heat up the iron and fuse it on down the rip. It'll work all right, I think."

"That's great!" I'm delighted. He's already wheeling out the door before I can thank him properly.

"When did he do that?" I ask Mom, helping her to sit up on the pillows.

"I don't know. It must have been the day you went off with Hector and I was lying here moaning and groaning—when was that?"

"Only yesterday, Mom."

"Only yesterday! It seems like . . . look, I'm hungry. I'm sick of lying here. I want to get up."

"No, Mom. You have to lie still for another day at least while the pills work."

"All right. But bring me food. Nice things. I want pizza and crayfish and oysters and a Jamaican curry with lots of coconut cream and then plenty of chocolate mousse and a meringue decorated with cherries soaked in Cointreau."

She has these fantasies. In the kitchen I make the baked vegetable casserole look prettier with a sprinkle of fresh basil and a tomato cut into the shape of a flower.

HECTOR

To pass some time I go down to the library to check a theory I have. I know the library well. I've read most of the books, but now I'm looking at them with altered eyes.

There's a large collection of books on the sciences: physics, mathematics, chemistry, medicine. There are books on philosophy and psychology. The history books cover wars, particularly the Second World War; there are also books about the British royal line. There's nothing about geography or any aspect of the physical world. There are several books on astronomy with charts of the stars and planets. There's nothing on animals or birds, mountains, trees, cities, houses, farms, or lakes. There are no pictures anywhere in any of these books.

But I do remember seeing pictures. Somewhere there must be pictures. I go to the children's section. It's in an alcove of its own with a red and yellow rug on the floor and small chairs shaped for children's bodies. It has been unused now for many years.

I go to the section for the very youngest. Now I can see at once that the books are handmade, the words drawn in ink in big letters, the pages stapled together at the side. The book I hold in my hands is about two little five-year-olds, a boy and a girl, Dagan and Astrid. One day they misbehave by talking too loudly and their voices boom through the tunnels and disturb all the people who are doing important work. They're punished and not allowed to eat dinner with everybody else in the big hall.

Here are the pictures I remembered. Drawings in the same ink but colored in, they're of children dressed in tunics, holding hands and staring off the pages with identical faces. They sit in an alcove like this one and look at books. There's one story I remember very well, about Astrid letting the angora rabbits out of their cages and they hop around the tunnels for a whole day. In another book Dagan and Astrid play with dogs like Stewart and climb up rocky walls like the ones I remember from the playroom in the nursery. As a special treat when they've been good, they're taken to see the kind Counselor and allowed to sit quietly and listen to his record player. There are no other books than books like these. So this was my childhood. The world was carefully filtered so I'd know of no other but this.

Far away at the end of the library I can see Estrella. She is sitting in the librarian's office, a room behind panels of sliding glass. She's only seven years older than I am, the next youngest to me. I haven't spoken to her since she was twelve and I was five, and she was taken away from the nursery to live with the women. She's pale and frail, her shoulders curved and her head hanging as if her neck cannot hold its weight. I think of my Diana, the strongest picture I have of her, striding out of the sky in her beautiful wings. Estrella's head lifts; she seems to be looking at me. I wave and smile at her, but she gives me no sign she's noticed I'm there.

Felix meets me as I leave the library and he walks

174

beside me through a side tunnel to my room. I distrust him now so much I can't even talk to him, but he seems to want to be silent himself, and just walks beside me until we reach my room. He comes in with me and sits on the chair by the desk.

"I need to check, Hector, that you have no ill effects from your visit to the outside."

He opens his bag, but instead of getting out medical gear it's the pen and paper again. "I'll take your blood pressure if I may," he says as he writes. He hands the paper to me. *I know you're going to leave again. When you do I want to come with you.*

I laugh. "No," I say in the loud voice I've learned in the outside world. "You can't take my blood pressure. I know the Counselor's sent you here. I know you're trying to help him. But you can't take my blood pressure. There's no way that I'll let you."

He understands that I am refusing to respond to his written message. He looks puzzled. He writes again and hands me the paper. *I'm on your side!* I laugh again and turn my back on him.

I refuse to read anything more he writes. He's been in on this from the beginning. He's going to help the Counselor. Of course I intend to get away from here again. At any moment now the poison will start filtering into the lake. I have to warn them.

DIANA

It's hot. Midafternoon and the heat's settling on the house like a burning iron. This morning there was a breeze. I did the final repairs on the wingset and took it for a flit around the lake, over the house and high enough to see the mountain, blue and tall without a fleck of snow. I landed again and went to find Dad.

He was still by the lake. He's been sitting there, near the blind, all night without moving as far as I know. It's almost as if he's speaking to the lake, or listening to it. I wanted to ask him to watch Mom while I flew to the clearing to check out Stewart. But Mom's okay on her own now, really. She's sitting up in bed reading now while I'm writing this, and she's looking quite normal. The wound on her leg has lost all the scary puffiness, and the redness has gone.

Dad didn't want to be disturbed this morning down at the lake. He said only that there's rain coming. He thinks it will rain tomorrow, and I looked to where he was pointing. Far to the south there was a wisp of cloud, like a tiny blemish on a pure blue tablecloth.

I flew to the clearing this morning. There was no Stewart. There was his bowl, licked clean, but no other sign of him. Just stillness, this oppressive heat building up. I landed, waited around, calling him. But there was no response.

<u>HECTOR</u>

Felix has gone, taking his pages of lies with him. I sit on my bed, plotting my escape. There's nothing much to plot. There's the guard to evade at the end of the tunnel leading to the maze, that's all. Not quite all. There's also a new booby trap that's been set up, whatever it is that triggers off the spotlight that hit Diana and me when we came through. That's new. It's been put in place since I left the last time.

There's a tap on my door and Jessyn comes in. He's carrying one of the plastic garments Diana and I had to wear. "The Counselor wants you to help," he says. "The pipeline is ready now. We have to be ready to help move the barrels of waste."

"Wearing these?" I ask, pointing at the plastic.

"We are moving the drums of toxic material first," he says, and then he leaves.

Jessyn is one of the men who've been guarding the entrance. I open my door and look out. Farther along the tunnel I see two figures already dressed in the plastic, shuffling off and around a bend. Another figure in plastic leaves a doorway. I can't tell who any of them are. I close my door and start putting on the plastic. It will act as a disguise. It's a gift.

I slip out of my room and hurry along the passage, keeping to the shadowy edges. I can move freely because I haven't zipped up the opening under my feet. I pass nobody. It seems everyone's gone to help far away in the system near the generator room. I creep farther along the endless tunnel to the wooden door marking the maze entrance. The door is unguarded.

Once I am through the door I start pulling off the plastic. I'm free again. But there is somebody here. I can see the old man standing with his little medical bag and long white beard. "Don't move," he says. It's Felix. He's the one who has been left on guard.

"I knew it," I say to him bitterly. "I knew you were spying on me. Working for the Counselor. I've always trusted you before, Felix, and now you—"

"Shut up," he hisses. "Or if you must continue your dramatic monologue, do it quietly. And don't take one more step from where you are. You have to walk very gently along here against the wall to where I'm standing. Otherwise you'll step on the trigger that sets off those confounded spotlights. Come on, now. This way. Very slowly."

I shut up and do as he says. I might as well. Things couldn't possibly be any worse, as Diana would say.

"Right," he says when I reach him. "Now come on, away from the light." The glow from the tunnel still reaches us. I follow him for a few minutes into the darkness toward the maze.

He's obviously been sent by the Counselor to follow me into the maze, to find the best point to blow it up with dynamite and block if off forever. I wonder where Stewart is. If he would only turn up now, I could push the old man over and run away with Stewart through the maze.

Felix stops and in the darkness I bump into him. He holds my arm. "Listen to me," he says, still whispering. "I am not spying on you for the Counselor, I'm spying on you for myself. I am coming with you to the outside. So lead on."

"Well," I say, shaking off his arm, talking to where I think his face is in the darkness, "you're not in luck.

I don't know the way through the maze to the outside. And even if I did, I wouldn't take you. Beth is probably dead now because of you. Because of your clever idea to send only one day's medication to her."

"My dear boy, that's not true." He sounds shocked. "I was *told* to send only one day's worth. But I packed up the whole course and the blood poison serum for an injection. Beth will be all right. The medication will have worked. I have great faith in Lark's research."

"But the Counselor told me, he said it was your idea—"

"Oh, the Counselor told you, did he?" He's still whispering, but his voice is loaded with meaning. I don't know what to believe. Felix goes on, "Didn't it occur to you that the Counselor would prefer that you not trust me?" He pauses. "Of course it wouldn't occur to you. You haven't been brought up to recognize such maneuvering. You've been taught to believe the Counselor at all times. Keep the children in innocence and you can manipulate an empire. Look, Hector, take me with you through the maze. You will see I am telling you the truth. Your little family by the lake will be safe, you'll see. I may be able to help Diana's father. And certainly I've brought enough medical supplies with me to make sure they remain safe once the lake becomes toxic."

"You know about the lake?"

"Oh, yes, I know about the lake. I've always known the Counselor would get the lake in the end, one way or another."

I tell him I can't lead him through the maze anyway, that I can't find the way without Stewart. I tell him I hadn't planned anything beyond getting past the guard. If I'd thought about the maze at all, it was with a feeble hope that miraculously Stewart would be there waiting for me.

Felix says that we'll have to do the best we can. I hear him open his bag. "I've got candles," he says, "and plenty of matches. Perhaps we'll manage." He lights a candle and holds it out for me to take, with a paper twisted into a cup shape at the base so the hot wax won't drip on my hand. He lights one for himself, closes his bag, and picks it up. "Come on," he says.

At first the tunnel is straight, easy to follow. After some time we come to the start of the maze. The first fork. "I don't know which way," I say before he can ask.

We take the left turning, which narrows and soon starts climbing. Then in the flicker from the candle I see the scratch on the wall. It's a definite *D*-shape, marked clearly at about eye level. I show Felix. "We're going the right way. Diana has left us a trail to follow."

Felix holds his candle up to the scratch on the wall. "You're sure Diana left these marks?"

"Of course," I say. "Come on." With all that's wrong, I'm happy. She must have left these marks for me.

We go a long way, twisting, climbing, passing other turnoffs, but always finding the next *D*. "It can't be much farther," I say to Felix. He's ahead of me. His candlelight has disappeared around a bend in the tunnel. "Felix?" I call.

"Stay there, Hector," I hear. "Just stay where you are."

I wait there for three or four seconds, held by his voice. I have time in those seconds to get many pictures of what it is he's found that he doesn't want me to see. The worst is of Diana, fallen, hurt, stranded in the maze, dying. I can't stand still. I go to Felix.

His candlelight falls on two bodies, two sets of bones. I can look for only an instant. As I turn away I remember most the glint of tarnished silver in the shreds of tunic, and the two heads together.

"It has to be Amy," Felix is saying. "Amy and John." He's kneeling, holding the candle in front of him. I can see the same glint of silver at the neck of his tunic and at the wrists, and the shine of tears on his face.

"After they left we waited. We didn't give up hope for months, some of us for years. So this is what happened to them." His voice is scratchy with grief.

For a long time he stays there. I slump down, leaning against the wall. I don't know what we should do now. I have seen that this tunnel doesn't go any farther.

"When they didn't return with rescuers and we heard nothing, gradually we came to believe in what the Counselor had been telling us. There must have been a nuclear war that had devastated the whole world. Nothing was left out there. There didn't seem to be any point in trying to get away. There didn't seem to be any point even in remembering what real life had been like. Our lives before coming underground became like dreams."

It is as if he is speaking to the two people whose bodies he kneels beside. "As the years went by and our lives went on, little by little we stopped talking to each other. It was too painful to recall our previous life and there was nothing else to talk about apart from work. Oh, yes, work went on in a halfhearted way. But the musicians gave up working quite soon—I can't remember the last time we had live music. The piano and the cello and the guitars and drums are moldering in the damp air. And Jock—you remember Jock, the painter? One day he refused to work anymore. He hasn't touched a brush for fifty years."

Felix's voice stops. Our candles flicker suddenly as if something had rushed by us. Half-afraid I watch the shadows leaping on the rocky wall. Then they are still again. It was nothing.

Finally Felix struggles to his feet. "Diana can't have gone on any farther this way," he says. His voice is normal again. "We might as well go back the way we came. We'll follow the *D*'s back to that first turnoff." He picks up a small stone. "We'll make our own marks along the walls. I want to remember where Amy and John are."

I can see he's tiring, becoming feebler. I take the stone from him and carry his bag for him too.

Then we hear the barking, and suddenly, galloping into the candlelight, there's Stewart. He's looking thin and his coat's dull, as if he's been waiting around the tunnels for days, but his tongue's lolling out and his eyes are bright. I tell Felix we're okay now.

DIANA

It's late afternoon. The heat has lifted and a breeze has arrived. The smudge of cloud in the south is turning golden as the sun moves down.

I get out the wingset again. On the grass waiting for me is a little backpack with rice cakes and milk for Stewart and the flashlight I've had on the recharger all day sticking out of the side pocket.

Dad comes wheeling toward me over the grass from the lake trail. His face looks tired but his eyes are steady. He says to me, "You won't go down to the tunnels, will you, Diana? You know if they catch you, they'll keep you there."

"I'm just taking some food for Stewart," I say, and I see his eyes on the flashlight, and he looks back at me, and I know that he knows that if I possibly can, I'll find Hector.

HECTOR

I thought all our problems were solved when Stewart found us. He led us back to the proper way out and started running ahead staying just inside the reaches of our candlelight. But we've gone no distance at all when he stops, looks back behind us, and grows tense.

Then Felix and I hear it too. They're coming after

us. We can hear the shouts and the thudding noise of feet rushing through the tunnels.

"Quick—Felix—we'll have to hide!" I say, but Felix's hand is on my arm holding me still.

"No," he says, "that's not anger, it's panic—" and as he speaks, someone appears around a curve in the tunnel, gasping, speaking incoherently. In the candlelight I see it's Lark, and then there are other people piling up behind her. Their faces are indistinct in the shadows, but I can see their eyes are wide and shiny with fear.

"The lake!" Lark is saying. "Hurry—we've got to keep moving—the lake's flooding through the tunnels!"

There is no time to argue or to find out more details. I shout "Follow us! Calm down and hold on to the person in front of you and just follow!" I've seen how big the lake is. It's a terrible thought, that huge volume of water swirling into these tunnels and trapping us here. I rush along behind Stewart, knowing all these people are following, and I pause only for a split second every ten paces or so to scratch a rough mark on the walls we're passing.

I hear Felix asking Lark if everyone's been saved. I can tell by his voice that his strength is nearly exhausted. He's a very old man, poor Felix. I don't hear Lark's reply. Right then my candle sputters and dies. It doesn't matter. We're there. The light from outside is filtering around the last few curves. Stewart is away ahead of me and his excited barking echoes back.

At last I'm outside. The cool dry air fills up my

lungs and I lean against the rocks for a few seconds with my eyes closed, just breathing.

My eyes have weakened again in the few days of living underground. I flicker them open just a little, but in that instant before I have to cover them from the fierce light I see in the sky the shape of Diana's wings. Probably I've imagined it. But the shape's still there behind my closed eyelids.

DIANA

I circle once above the clearing. It's deserted as before, but now with deep shadows thrown by the setting sun. I circle again lower. I'll leave the food for Stewart. Perhaps he'll come back and find it.

I swoop lower, deciding where to land, and there is Stewart! He just appears out of the rocks. Then Hector is there too. "Hector!" I scream, hitting the ground and unbuckling the harness faster than I ever have before. He's really here. I don't know if he saw me or not. He has his hands over his eyes in the way I remember. As I run toward him, I'm aware there are all these people crawling out of the rock behind him, but right now I don't take any notice. I throw my arms around his neck.

I hear someone say "All right, you two," and there's Felix squinting at me through his fingers. "Felix," I say, "you saved Mom. She's okay!" Then I can no longer avoid noticing the other people. At first they all look the same to me. Pale hands shielding pale faces from the light, exhausted bodies dressed in white tunics, thin pale ankles disappearing into cloth slippers. I hear Hector's voice in my ear. "They say the lake's flooding out the tunnels."

I pull back and stare at him. I can hardly understand what he's saying to me.

"It's true," he says. "That's why they're all here."

He's looking around, seems to be counting. People are still stumbling from the maze entrance. The first ones are spreading out over the clearing. The light's fading. Gradually they are taking their hands from their eyes and they can see.

"There are only about forty," Hector says to Felix. "The rest must be trapped down there."

Felix doesn't seem to be listening. He's looking at the trees around the clearing and at the sky.

"Is this it?" someone says to Felix. "Is this really the outside?" He's still not listening to anybody, just looking.

I'm staying close to Hector. Again, seeing so many people at once makes me uneasy. But it's not as bad as it was in the dining hall. That's probably because this time they're not staring at me. They're taking no notice of me at all. They're gazing at the sky, fingering the branches of the trees and the leaves and stooping to touch the soft moss on the floor of the clearing. They are still, eyes closed, taking deep breaths of air.

"Yes," someone standing behind me says. "We're outside." I turn around. It's an old lady, as old as Felix perhaps, a pale, lined face with white hair coiled on top of her head. She's got the silver threads running through the embroidery at her neck. Hector once told me the silver in the embroidery is reserved for the tunics of the "originals," the people who came from the outside to live in the community when it began.

"This is Anna," Hector says to me, and she says she knows who I am because she saw me the other day in the big hall. "And this is Estrella," Hector says. She's standing beside Anna, almost leaning on her. Estrella is so thin, I wonder how she can stand upright. She has big dark eyes and black hair falling on her shoulders, and she stares at me for a moment and then she smiles. Now that I am starting to see these people one by one, it's easier for me to cope with them. I realize they'll be able to come and live with us near the lake, and we'll have a real town.

But they're talking about the lake as if it has somehow emptied itself into the underground tunnels, as if someone has pulled out a bath plug. "We were connecting the last pipe," a blond man was saying to Hector and Felix. "There was a terrific rumbling sound and the ground shook—we just ran."

"We shouted to everyone to try and get out," another man said. "I looked back and there was water shooting everywhere. It was tumbling through the pipes. Pushing them aside like matchsticks."

"We were in the dining hall and heard the shouting," Lark says. "We looked out and they were running toward us. It was as if a wall of water was chasing them."

"There was no time to think," the first man says. "We all headed for the maze. We knew you had gotten out this way once before, Hector."

"I can't understand it," Hector says. "Why would the lake source suddenly flood like that? Rivers can't turn around and start running backward, can they?"

The blond man shrugs. "It might have been a little earthquake, perhaps, causing a slight shift of water levels. I really cannot explain it."

"It's not an ordinary lake," I say. They turn to look at me as if I've said something unusual. It's what Dad used to say as he told me stories about the lake and the people like old McGregor who lived there, and how the birds stayed alive there when everywhere else they were dying. "You must remember, Diana," he'd say, "it's not an ordinary lake."

"Well," Hector says uncertainly, "the thing is, over half of our people are still down there." Nobody replies. It's clear everybody is expecting him to take charge. "I'll go back down," he continues, sounding more confident, "and see what's happened."

There's a flutter of breaths like sighs of relief from the silent people. I was right; they do want Hector to take over and tell them what to do. They seem to have no wills of their own.

"Okay, then." Hector looks around. "Where is Stewart?"

Stewart's nose is resting on my little shoulder pack on the ground by my wingset. "He's starving," I say. "Give him a chance to eat first."

Hector whispers to me while I'm feeding Stewart. "Will you stay here and, you know, sort of keep an eye on everybody?"

"No!" I say. "I'm not staying here on my own with all these people! I'm coming with you."

"They won't hurt you, Diana. Look, they've never been outside before. They won't know what to expect when it gets dark and everything—"

"They'll be all right. Felix is here, anyway. I'm coming with you, Hector, and that's that."

HECTOR

She said she was coming back underground with me and there was no way I could talk her out of it. Lark is with us too. We didn't discuss it, but I know she's coming in case we find injured people. She's got Felix's medical bag.

We go down through the maze cautiously at first, and then more quickly as we find no floodwaters rising to meet us. It's easier too with the strong beam from Diana's flashlight. In no time at all, it seems, we're standing at the entrance to the main tunnels.

"The lights are still working," Lark says. "I did not expect that the generator would be unaffected."

"Nothing's changed at all," Diana says as we walk on through the tunnels. She flashes her light around. "I can't see any sign of this tidal wave."

"Yes, there is," Lark says suddenly. She steadies Diana's aimlessly swinging flashlight and directs the beam ahead of us. We're getting close to the big dining hall.

The rock walls are dripping and puddles of water lie

on the ground. Chairs from the big hall are washed against the sides of the tunnel. There's a little shoal of cups resting in a doorway, a trail of smashed glass leading around a corner. The only sound comes from the *plink-plonk* of drops of water falling from the curving walls into the pools on the ground.

"Well," says Diana less confidently, "it smells just as bad as before, even if everything has been washed."

That reminds me. "Lark, what about the toxic waste? They hadn't started pouring it into the pipeline, had they?" If they had started, then I knew the lake would be poisoned already, and the poison would also be concentrated in the pools on the ground and hanging in the air as a gas. The chief engineer had told us the pipeline was smashed apart by the force of the water.

"No," Lark says. "They were waiting around to start, but the Counselor did not want the pouring to begin until the last pipe was laid."

"Hang on a minute," Diana interrupts. "What are you two saying? You mean you were going to chuck that poison junk into the lake source anyway? Even though I didn't bring back a pump?"

I hadn't intended that Diana should find that out. I start to tell her that it was going to be buried somewhere, but I'm not good at lying, and she interrupts again almost immediately.

"I want to know the truth! I hate it when people keep things from me. Look, Hector, it's just like Mom and Dad telling me for years that everyone's up there on the moon waiting to come back someday and then

I hear Mom telling you it's all lies! They just told me it was true to keep me happy!"

I remember Beth telling me that it was unlikely everyone could be living safely on the moon. I didn't know Diana had overheard, and even if I had known, I wouldn't have realized she would be so upset about it.

Meanwhile Lark is looking at the two of us with her eyes wide with disbelief. "People on the moon?" she's asking. "You mean there might be people walking around on the moon?"

"We don't know for sure," I tell Lark. "I mean to say, yes, they say there have been people up there, but—" I stop. This conversation is getting out of control. "Can't we talk about all of this later?"

I see Diana and Lark exchange a glance. It puzzles me. Diana seems to create undercurrents of meaning and I always feel a step behind. Fortunately we've got a job to do. We're busy here. I get things organized again.

"Right," I say. "Let's keep going. Don't forget we're here to rescue people." I walk along the tunnel so it's quite clear I don't care if they look at each other again.

DIANA

We find the people. They're shocked, but no one is hurt. Well, I think they're shocked. They sit in the huge dining hall on the chairs that the floodwater didn't smash or hurl out into the passageway. The people are absolutely silent, not looking at each other. But then that's what these people are like all the time down here. At first they don't even look at Lark and Hector, and there's no sign that they're pleased to see them.

However, after a little while, one by one they start to speak.

I notice that many of them are old, as old as Felix. They wear the tunics with the silver embroidery. There's also a group of younger people who, it appears, were dressed in the plastic envelopes and were in the storeroom by the generator waiting for the instruction to start disposing of the toxic material. Once again I'm intimidated by this mass of people, and beyond picking out those two groups I can't distinguish them as individuals yet.

It seems most of the old ones were in their rooms when the panic started. When they heard the shouting and the roaring waters, they shut their doors and barricaded them and put their heads under their pillows till it stopped.

But now they hear from Lark that nearly half of the underground community escaped up through the maze and they are this very moment in the outside world. They turn to each other for the first time, and there's a whisper fluttering around—*outside*. It has a regretful sound, as if they're thinking about what they've missed.

One of them tells Lark that she looked outside her door as the smashing noise of the floodwaters receded. "I glimpsed it," she says, "just for a second as it went past one of the tunnel lamps."

"*It?*" asks Lark.

"Like a pillar of swirling water," the woman says. "No, more like a monster rushing around the curve in the tunnel. A giant made of water."

She looks around but the other people won't meet her eyes and she stops speaking and bows her head, as if she's embarrassed. She mutters, "It must have been a trick of the light."

I notice the man called Jessyn, whom I remember from the last time I was here. He must have come in while we were listening to the woman speak. I'm sure I would have seen him earlier if he'd been here all along.

"I have searched through the whole system. There is nobody now remaining in any of the rooms," he says to Lark and Hector.

"That will be correct, Jessyn," Lark says. How formally these people speak to each other. "I have counted sixty-two here including you, Jessyn, and there are thirty-nine outside including Hector and myself but excluding you, Diana."

"That's only 101. I thought you told me there were 102 people here, Hector?"

Nobody answers me at first and in the short silence I work out for myself who's missing.

"Did you check the Counselor's room, Jessyn?" Hector asks.

"No, I did not. The door was closed. I assumed he would not want to assemble in the dining hall with the rest of us."

"Quite so," Lark says.

I get the impression they're uneasy. In the moment

of silence I hear the slight click of Stewart's claws and I look around to see him disappearing through a door at the side of the dining hall. Nobody's watching me. I slip through the door after him, unnoticed.

I'm in a huge kitchen. Here, for once, the pervasive fumes are defeated by a whole range of new but much nicer smells. The best one comes from a wire basket filled with globes the size of my fist and a glossy golden-brown. I poke one of them with my finger. At first it seems hard but then the crusty outer surface gives way with a series of snaps. This must be bread. Mom has spoken longingly about bread.

Stewart has his paws up on a bench and his nose is thrusting toward a big pan. I lift the cover off. What's inside doesn't smell exactly unpleasant but it is strong—much too overpowering. I couldn't imagine being able to eat it. Stewart obviously thinks it's a great smell. Perhaps it's dog food. I'm considering giving him some when Hector comes in.

"Is this for Stewart's dinner?" I ask him, pointing inside the pan.

"No, not exactly. It's—well, never mind now, I'll tell you later. Look, Diana, this flood or wave of water or whatever—apparently it raced along the main corridors, swirled around the dining hall for a second or two, then sort of drained away. What I want to know is, is that normal? I mean, have you ever seen anything like that?"

I think what Hector's trying to say is: Is this yet another bizarre phenomenon of the outside world he has yet to find out about? I shake my head.

"Well," he goes on, "Jessyn says the gardens are okay, the generator's untouched, the ducks and chickens and rabbits are fine—"

"You've got *rabbits*? Show me."

"Not right now. Look, we've got to decide what to do with all these people!"

"What do you mean—do with them?"

"There's that group in there wondering what's going on outside and those others outside wondering what's going on down here. And I know Felix wants to leave the caves forever and Lark as well—"

"It's quite simple, Hector. Just tell the people in the dining hall they can either stay here or they can come with us back to the lake. Easy. And Hector—can we take some bread back for Mom?"

HECTOR

Diana really doesn't know the first thing about these people down here. Let them choose, she says. She doesn't realize that in all our lives here we've never made a decision about anything. Even the simplest choices like what clothes to wear or what food to eat are already made for us. So when I stand up in front of the group in the dining hall, it's with the pessimistic feeling that my words are not going to help anyone.

"Lark and Diana and I are going back through the maze to tell the people outside that you are all safe and that everything down here is okay. Then we're not coming back here. We're going to Diana's place."

There's no response, not a murmur. "Some of the others up there might come with us or they might come back down here. We don't know. So you can all decide for yourselves. You can stay here or come with us."

The silence goes on. Nobody moves. They're not even looking at me. It's as I thought. A decision is too difficult. I understand. I was one of them not so long ago.

Diana speaks from where she's standing by the door. "You don't have to make a final choice right now. After all, Hector's marked the way through the maze now. You can stay here if you wish and go outside later. If you don't like it out there you can come back to the caves as soon as you want to. You can come and go as you please."

A voice comes from the back of the group. "We cannot do that. He would never allow it."

Diana walks over to where Lark and I stand. "It's the Counselor they're thinking about," she whispers. "He's got them all paralyzed."

She's right. We're afraid of him. Most of the people in the caves don't ever see him, and yet his power is in their minds all the time.

"He's got to be told," Diana says, "that he hasn't got any right to imprison people."

Her voice is loud enough now for everyone to hear. I see their heads lifting and their eyes focusing on her.

"And I think we should go and tell him," she finishes.

It is the thought of the power he has always wielded

from the separate stronghold of his room that keeps us in fear. In reality, I know now, he's just a sick old man whose mind is not stable.

"Come on, Hector, let's go and tell him," Diana urges. "Come with us, Lark." She goes toward the door. I find myself following her. I can hear a suppressed murmur of something like excitement from the people. I look back. They're watching us. Lark is also moving toward the door with us.

Without speaking, the three of us go toward the Counselor's room. We're walking carefully to avoid the puddles and wreckage left by the floodwater. Debris that was swept up by the water has been left in drifts in doorways or caught against the rocky walls. A teaspoon balanced on one of the lamp-holders flashes in the beam from Diana's flashlight.

To distract my mind from dwelling unpleasantly on confronting the Counselor, I remember the way Diana's nose wrinkled as she smelt the pan of rabbit stew in the kitchen. She wouldn't have any idea what it was. The Redferns never eat meat.

We reach the Counselor's room. For the first time, in the strong light thrown by the torch, I see the delicate gold tracery in the carvings on his door. I'm wondering which of us will do the talking when we get inside. "Come on, then," Diana whispers.

Lark stops her. She holds Diana's arms and talks to her softly but with great intensity. "Do not let him look at you," she says. "Do not shine the light on him. You *must not* see his eyes."

Diana looks at Lark for a long moment. Then she

steps forward and uses the flashlight to push the door open.

It swings noiselessly. Inside the room there is absolute darkness. We stand at the doorway. Diana is holding the light low, sweeping it along the floor. She steps inside the room hesitantly, and Lark and I follow.

The thick carpet squelches under our feet. The flashlight beam touches the papers that I had seen lying on the table, the plans and the drawings for the pipeline excavations. They have been swept onto the floor and the ink on the drawings is smudged and washed away. The heavy velvet drapes that I see for the first time in the light hang heavy and sodden. The floodwaters have been in this room.

The flashlight reaches the Counselor, shows the gleaming hem of his tunic clinging wetly around his ankles. Slowly Diana moves the light upward. His knees. His hands resting on the open book. His arms. "Not his face!" Lark's voice hisses. "I do not want to see his eyes—"

Diana takes no notice. There is his face in the glow of the flashlight. There is no need to worry about his eyes anymore. They're wide open and staring at us, but they're dead. He's dead. His mouth is frozen into a stretch of fear. Drops of water still glisten in his beard.

We go away and close the door quietly behind us.

DIANA

"The Counselor is dead."

I watch the faces in the dining hall as Hector says the words.

I suppose I expect cheers and clapping. Nothing happens. They simply sit and wait.

Finally Jessyn speaks. "So you are now the Counselor, Hector."

"No," Hector says. "Don't you understand—*there is no Counselor*. It's over."

I wish Felix were here. He'd show some feelings.

"We'll have to go," Hector says to Lark and me. "They'll be wondering what has happened to us."

Then someone says, "You are really going to the outside world?"

"Is it really still there?" someone else asks. "Would we see trees and the sky?"

"Well, it'll be dark by now," Hector says.

"There's a full moon tonight," I remind him.

"Is it far?" somebody asks.

"We have to go through the maze," Hector tells them, "which is steep and narrow in places." He hesitates, and I think he's realizing that many of these people are old and that the climb might be too much for them—particularly after everything else that has happened today. "It might be better if you stay here tonight—after all, you can leave here anytime you like—"

"No." An elderly man interrupts him. "I will not wait any longer. I want to see the world once more."

"So do I," someone else says.

"I am coming too," another voice joins in. "Even if I drop down dead in the attempt, I want to see the outside."

In the end they all come. A curious procession sets off through the maze. Some carry candles, others are tottering on walking sticks. Hector and I lead the way with Stewart and the flashlight. Jessyn and Lark are at the end.

"Have you considered," Hector asks me, "what we will do if they all decide to come with us to Redfern Lake tonight?"

"What we will do? We'll all be walking very slowly, that's what."

"That's not what I mean, stupid. What would we do with them once we got there? What would Beth and Evan think?"

"They'd think it was great. It's New Year's Eve, isn't it? What's a few extra guests at a New Year's Eve party?" I won't answer his questions seriously. It's better to wait and see what happens.

Hector drops back to help people up a steep part of the tunnel. I continue ahead with Stewart, wondering if Hector's parents are in our procession. It's odd the way he won't talk about them. I remember the strange thing that I noticed when Lark was holding my arm and speaking to me so intensely before we went into the Counselor's room. Just for a second she looked exactly like Hector. A particular fleeting movement of her eyebrows—something like that, I suppose. The next second it was gone. But the resemblance had been there, strong enough to make me wonder if Lark is Hector's mother. If so, why the big secret? There are so many mysterious things about these people.

At long last Stewart and I get to the outside. It's a beautiful night, silver and blue, with the round moon rising. There is the right amount of light for the people we've brought out this time to see the clearing, the others waiting for us, the outline of the trees, the sky, the stars.

I can see the bank of cloud building across the base of the moon. Dad was right; it will rain, if not tomorrow, then sometime soon.

Lark finds me where I am sitting beside Felix, leaning against the rocks and watching the moon. "Is it possible, Diana, that there are people up there on the moon, waiting to come back?"

"Perhaps. I really don't know," I reply. Right now I feel I've found all the new people I could want. They're a strange and silent sort, but then so was Hector at first.

Someone's voice breaks the eerie hush in the clearing. "It's after midnight. Two thousand twenty-five is over. It's the first day of 2026."

Someone cheers, softly, creakily, in a voice that for years has done no more than whisper in the caves. It's as if they are now fully aware they are released from the hypnotic influence of the Counselor. Someone else laughs, and gradually the sense of liberation spreads until everyone is laughing and calling "Happy New

Year!" and whistling and cheering into the night. They are free. It's their new world—or their old world.

A little while later Hector, Stewart, and I are walking alone through the moonlight back to the lake. The others have gone back to the caves to prepare to leave them forever. They're coming to live with us near the lake. I would have liked the drama of presenting Mom and Dad with a hundred new people in the middle of the night. But I suppose Hector was right. It would have been a long and grueling walk for the cave people tonight.

Mom and Dad will be waiting up for me, I know. We'll have a lot to talk about. After all, we've got a whole new town to plan.

"You'll be able to feel what rain is like, Hector," I say. He replies after a moment, "And I'll learn to fly."

But mostly we walk in silence. I don't know where Hector's thoughts are. As for mine, I'm shaping the words for my diary: the story of the lake and the underground tunnels.